B B  N

MW00465342

PRAYING FOR RAIN

Copyright © 2019 by BB Easton
Published by Art by Easton
All rights reserved.

ISBN: 978-1-7327007-2-7
e-book ISBN: 978-1-7327007-3-4

Cover Design by BB Easton
Cover Photographs licensed by Shutterstock
Content Editing by Traci Finlay and Karla Nellenbach
Copyediting by Jovana Shirley of Unforeseen Editing
and Ellie McLove of My Brother's Editor
Formatting by Jovana Shirley of Unforeseen Editing

No part of this book may be reproduced or transmitted in any
form or by any means, electronic or mechanical, including
photocopying, recording, or by any information storage and
retrieval system without the written permission of the author,
except for the use of brief quotations in a book review.

This is a work of fiction, and any resemblance to persons,
living or dead, places, or actual events is purely coincidental.
The characters and locale are products of the author's
imagination and are used fictitiously. The publisher and author
acknowledge the trademark status and trademark ownership of
all trademarks, service marks, and word marks mentioned in
this book.

Due to themes of drug abuse, graphic violence, and explicit
sexual content, this book is not intended for anyone under the
age of eighteen.

This book is dedicated to anyone who needs a reminder that none of this matters, and we're all going to die.

And also to T.M. Frazier, who is in charge of reminding me.

CHAPTER 1

Rain

I'M SITTING IN A booth at Burger Palace. I don't remember how I got here, or when, but the empty seat across from me tells me that I came alone.

The place smells like classic greasy burgers and fries. My stomach snarls in response.

God, I'm starving.

I glance across the bustling fast-food restaurant at the giant digital menu on the wall and notice four banners hanging on either side of the checkout counter. They're huge, hanging from the ceiling all the way down to the floor. Only, instead of showing pretty models eating airbrushed cheeseburgers, these things look like propaganda for the Antichrist. Each one is bright red with the silhouette of a hooded figure on horseback in the middle. One is holding a massive sword over his head. Another one has a scythe, like the Grim Reaper. One is swinging a mace, and the fourth one is charging forward with a flaming torch. Even though I can't see their faces, I almost feel like their demonic eyes are staring right at me.

This is a fucked up marketing campaign, *I think, searching the terrifying banners for more information.*

The only text I see on them anywhere is a simple date in bold white font at the top of each one.

April 23.

What the hell?

I look around the restaurant for more clues, but all I find are happy little families sucking soda out of red cups with hooded horsemen on them. A little boy carries a Big Kid Box to his seat with an image of the Grim Reaper guy on it. A little girl licks blood-red ice cream out of a cracked black cone. And, on every wrapper, every poster, every napkin, straw, and ketchup packet, there's the same date.

April 23? *I rack my brain.* April 23. What the hell is going to happen on April twen—

Before I can finish my thought, the lights flicker off and the doors burst open. Wind whips through the small restaurant like a tornado, sending drinks crashing and people scrambling, as four hooded figures on giant smoke-breathing horses charge in.

Suddenly, the banners, the ad campaign—it all makes sense.

Today is April 23.

And we're all gonna die.

Smoke and screams and chaos fill the air as I scurry to the floor beneath my table, backing all the way up to the wall and hugging my knees to my chest.

I can't breathe. I can't blink. I can't think. All I can do it cover my ears and try to block out the screams of mothers and children as I peer into the darkness.

Flames climb up the black-and-red banners, illuminating a wasteland before me. Furniture overturned. Bodies strewed about the wreckage. Severed heads, missing limbs, torsos impaled on table legs. My hands move from my ears to my mouth as I muffle a scream.

Don't let them hear you.

Thick black smoke begins to curl and creep into my hiding spot, making my eyes water and my throat burn. I can hardly see past the table now, and suppressing the cough and the panic building in my throat is getting harder and harder to do.

I know I need to run—I have to—but my legs won't cooperate. I'm stuck in the fetal position, rocking like a child, as I pull my T-shirt over my mouth and nose.

I scream at myself inside my head, but it's my mother's voice that finally gets my ass in gear. "Are you going to stay home all day and wallow, like your father, or are you gonna get out there and try to help somebody?" *Her scolding from this morning rings in my ears louder than the cries of the burning, impaled women and children all around me.*

I want to help. Even if, right now, the only person I can help is myself.

Placing my palms on the filthy floor, I slowly bring my knees down so that I'm on all fours.

I can do this.

Taking one last breath, I straighten my back and prepare to crawl to safety. I can't see the exits through all the smoke, but I can see the two blood-spattered hooves that come to a stop directly in front of me when I take my first step.

I wake up at the tail end of a scream, just like I do every morning. Just like we all do, ever since the nightmares began.

Grabbing my cell phone off the charger, I hold my breath and read the date.

April 20.

I sigh and toss it back onto the nightstand.

I used to feel so relieved when I woke up from the nightmare. Back when I still had hope that some scientist somewhere was gonna figure it out. But everybody on the planet has been dreaming about the four horsemen of the apocalypse coming on April 23 for almost a year now, and we still don't have answers.

After a few months, most of the world's top researchers either resigned in defeat, died from heart attacks, or went crazy from the stress of trying to figure it out. Every day, the news got worse, the crime rate skyrocketed, and eventually, the newscasters just stopped reporting. Without answers or hope or, hell, even fake news to calm us down, most people have just accepted that the world is going to end on April 23.

Myself included.

I still feel relieved when I wake up from the nightmare, but now, it's only because I can't wait for it to be over.

Three more days. I only have to do this shit for three more days.

I drag myself out of bed and groan at my reflection in the bathroom mirror. Choppy, chin-length black hair frames my pale face, the same way that yesterday's smudged eyeliner frames my sunken blue eyes.

Where the fuck did my hair go?

My eyes scan the filthy countertop for a brush and land on my long black braid, still bound with an elastic band, lying in a heap next to an empty bottle of codeine cough syrup.

Way to go, Rain. Get high and cut all your hair off. Real original.

I try to remember what happened last night, but it's not even a blur. It's just gone. Like the hair that I pick up and toss onto my overflowing trash can on my way to turn on the shower.

We've been advised to use our bathtubs for water storage in case our town's supply gets cut off, but the way I see it, if we're all going to die anyway, why not enjoy a hot shower first?

And by *enjoy*, I mean cry under the stream until the water turns cold.

I towel-dry my hack job of a hairdo, throw on a tank top and a pair of plaid flannel pajama pants, and shove my feet into an old pair of cowboy boots. I used to want to look cute when I left the house. Now, I just want to look homeless. Bronzer, beachy waves, cleavage, cutoff jeans—all those things attract attention. The bad kind. The kind that gets you robbed or raped. At least, around here.

As much as I'd like to spend the next three days in bed with my head under the covers, I'm fucking starving, and all we have here is dried spaghetti noodles, a can of lima beans, and a bottle of expired pancake syrup. Our supplies have been running low ever since the gangs took over the neighborhood grocery stores. They'll let you *shop*, but you have to be willing to pay in their *preferred currency*, which, when you're a nineteen-year-old girl...

Let's just say I haven't gotten that desperate yet.

Luckily, Burger Palace is still serving. And *they* take cash. I just have to get in and out without drawing too much attention to myself.

I pick the Twenty One Pilots hoodie up off my floor and resist the urge to bury my nose in the soft cotton like I used to. I know Carter's scent is long gone, just like him—and thank God for that. The last thing I need is another reminder that my stupid boyfriend chose to spend his last few weeks on earth in Tennessee with his family instead of here with me.

Asshole.

I yank the sweatshirt on over my head, completing my frumpiest look yet, and stomp down the stairs. The scene in the living room is pretty much the same as it is every morning. My father is passed out in his recliner, facing the front door, with a fifth of whiskey tucked in the crook of his elbow and a shotgun across his lap. I'd probably take more pity on him if he hadn't always been a mean-ass drunk.

But he has.

He's just a *paranoid* mean-ass drunk now.

I can't even bear to look at him. I cover my mouth with the sleeve of my sweatshirt to keep from gagging on the smell of piss as I snatch his prescription bottle of hydrocodone off the table.

I think you've had enough, old man.

Popping one of the little white pills into my mouth, I pocket the rest and cross the living room.

I grab my dad's keys off the hook by the front door and lock the doorknob on my way out. Even though I know how to drive, I don't bother taking my dad's truck. The roads are so clogged with wrecked and abandoned vehicles that they're basically impassable now.

Traffic laws were one of the first things to go after the nightmares began. Everybody started driving a little faster, having a few extra drinks, ignoring those pesky red lights and stop signs, and forgetting that turn signals had ever existed. There were so many accidents that the tow trucks and traffic cops and ambulance drivers couldn't keep up, so eventually, they just quit trying. The wrecks piled up and caused more wrecks, and then, when the gas stations closed, people started leaving their vehicles wherever they ran out of gas.

Franklin Springs, Georgia, has never exactly been a classy place, but now, it looks like one big demolition derby arena. I would know. I live right off the main two-lane highway that cuts through town. In fact, the *Welcome to Franklin Springs* sign hangs right across the street from my house. Of course, somebody recently spray-painted a giant UC over the RAN in Franklin, so the sign reads *Welcome to Fucklin Springs* now.

Can't imagine who would do such a thing.

The quickest way into town would be to walk along the highway about a mile or so, but it also feels like the quickest way to get raped or robbed, frumpy outfit or not, so I stick to the woods.

As soon as my feet hit the pine needle–covered trail behind my house, I feel like I can finally relax. I inhale the humid spring air. I listen to the birds chattering away up in the trees. I try on a smile; it doesn't feel right. And I pretend, for just a moment, that everything's okay again, like it used to be.

But, when I step out of the woods and feel the heat of a nearby car fire on my face, I remember.

Life sucks, and we're all gonna die.

I flip my hood over my head and tiptoe around the corner of the library, watching out for the three Rs: rioters, rapists, and rabid dogs. The dogs don't really have rabies, but so many people have died in the weeks leading up to April 23 that their pets are starting to band together and hunt as a team.

So. Many. People.

Images of those I've lost flicker behind my eyes, dim and grainy, fighting to get a feeling past the hydrocodone. But the painkiller does its job, and within moments, I'm fuzzy and numb again.

When the coast is clear, I shove my hands in the front pocket of my hoodie to keep all my shit from falling out and scurry across the street. Cars and trucks are lurched on the curbs, overturned in the ditches, and abandoned with doors wide open in the middle of the lanes. I try not to think about how many of those cars might still have people in them as I reach out and pull open the Burger Palace door.

When I walk in, I half-expect to see flaming banners and demons slaying people on horseback, but it's just the entire miserable town of Franklin, crammed inside and yelling at each other.

God, it's loud. People who've lived here their whole lives are shoving fingers in each other's faces, arguing about who was next in line. Babies are crying. Mothers are crying. Toddlers are screaming and running around like wild animals. And everybody smells like liquor.

I sigh and begin to make my way to the back of the line when I notice that my third-grade teacher, Mrs. Frazier, is standing at a cash register. It's her turn to order, but she's too busy cursing out Pastor Blankenship, who's behind her in line, to get on with it. I'm sure Mrs. Frazier wouldn't mind if I—

I slip in front of her at the cash register, hoping she keeps screaming long enough for me to order.

"Hi, and welcome to Burger Palace!" A girl wearing a Burger Palace cap and polo shirt beams at me from across the counter. "May I take your order?"

I glance down the line and notice three more employees, all sporting the same exaggerated grin.

What the hell are they giving these people? Molly? Crystal meth?

"Uh … yeah." I keep my voice low. "I'll have a soda and a large fry."

"Would you like to Apocasize that?"

I blink. Twice. "I'm sorry, what?"

"Apocasize it!" She gestures up at one of the digital screens behind her, where an animated thirty-two-ounce drink and bucket of fries are holding hands and skipping around a fire. "It's not like we have to worry about carbs anymore, am I right?"

My eyebrows pull together. "Uh … no, I guess not." I hear Mrs. Frazier call Pastor Blankenship a cunt behind me and know I'd better wrap it up. "Sure, whatever. How much does that cost?"

Perky Polly on Molly taps her monitor a few times. "That'll be forty-seven fifty."

"For a soda and fries?" I blurt.

She shrugs, never letting her smile slip.

"Jesus," I mutter under my breath as I dig in my hoodie pocket for some cash.

Price-gouging pieces of—

I set the contents of my pocket on the counter to sort through them, and with that one simple, absentminded gesture, all holy hell breaks loose. Perky Polly leaps across the counter, clawing at my little orange prescription bottle, at the exact same moment that Pastor Blankenship swipes one long arm out to grab it. Their fists collide, knocking the plastic bottle to the floor, which I manage to get a foot on before it can roll away. But, as I kneel down to pick it up, Mrs. Frazier launches herself at my back and sends us both crashing into the counter.

The entire crowd surges forward, pinning us to the stainless steel surface as they push and pull and claw at the salvation in my fist with greedy, desperate hands. I scream as one of them rips out a chunk of my hair. I hiss as another rakes her nails across my cheek. I bite and elbow as many others as I can. Howls and grunts and frustrated curses pour out of me as I struggle against the mob. The weight of them is crushing, pushing me down. I curl into a ball on the floor, clutching the bottle to my chest with both fists as I wince and take their beating.

Then, just as suddenly as it began, it stops. The ringing in my ears registers a moment later. Someone fired a gun. Or a freaking cannon from the sound of it.

The room goes quiet, and the crowd freezes, but I don't look up.

It could be a trick. It could be somebody just trying to distract me so that somebody else can snatch my pills. It could be—

I wince as the hot metal muzzle of a gun sears my temple.

"I'll be taking this." I hear the stranger's voice just before a firm hand wraps around my upper arm and yanks me to my feet.

I stand in a daze and face my attackers. They don't even have the decency to look ashamed. In fact, they don't look at me at all. Their eyes, a few pistols, and at least one rifle are all trained on the person holding a gun to my head. They're not mad that he's about to kidnap me. They're mad that he's kidnapping my pills.

"Who the hell are you?" Mr. Lathan, our former postman, growls from the back of the crowd. One of his eyes is squeezed shut as he stares down the length of his rifle, ready to fire.

My abductor shrugs as he walks me backward toward the door. "Doesn't really matter, does it?"

I watch the glow of anger in everyone's eyes cloud over with despair as they take in the meaning of his words.

Today is April twentieth. Nothing matters anymore.

I don't struggle. I don't even turn around and look at him. I let him drag me behind the building and pray that, whatever he does, he does it quick.

So much for not drawing attention.

I realize along the way that I'm limping, but I can't seem to pin down the location of my injury. And my mouth tastes like blood, but it doesn't hurt. And my body feels all floaty and light even though I just got jumped by half the town.

Damn, this hydrocodone is some powerful shit.

I giggle at the absurdity of my situation as the gunman behind me guides me toward a parked dirt bike with the heel of his palm on my shoulder.

"What's so funny?" His voice is soft, just like his touch as we come to a stop.

I turn to answer him and almost choke on my own spit. The words dry up in my mouth as I stare into the mossy-green eyes of a guy not much older than me. A tall, gorgeous guy who should be on a poster in my bedroom, not kidnapping me from Burger Palace.

I expected my captor to be some middle-aged, beer-gutted, gray-bearded, bald guy, not ... *this*. *This* guy is perfect. It's like his parents were so rich that they went to the doctor and selected his DNA from a menu before he was conceived— high cheekbones, straight nose, soft eyes, strong eyebrows, and full lips that he's chewing on absentmindedly.

But the rest of him doesn't look rich at all. He's wearing a white ribbed tank top under a blue floral Hawaiian shirt, his jeans have holes in them, and the disheveled brown hair tucked behind his ear looks like it hasn't seen a pair of scissors in years.

Mine, on the other hand ...

I run my fingers through my hacked-off locks, suddenly feeling super self-conscious about my frumpalicious appearance.

My captor raises his dark eyebrows a little higher, indicating that he's still waiting for me to tell him what's so funny.

I think about the painkillers that made me giggle, which causes me to remember all the other stuff I pulled out of my pocket along with that little orange bottle. "Shit!" I gasp, frantically patting my lower belly, feeling for the contents of my hoodie pocket. "I left all my money on the counter in there! And my keys!" I grimace and pinch the bridge of my nose. "God, I'm such an idiot."

"You still got those pills?" The boy pulls back one side of his unbuttoned Hawaiian shirt and shoves his handgun into a brown leather holster.

"Uh ... yeah ..." I wrap my fist a little tighter around the plastic bottle.

"Good." He flicks his chin toward the dirt bike behind me. "Get on."

"Where are we going?"

He lets his shirt fall back into place and pins me with a look that I can't quite read. It's been so long since I've seen somebody display anything other than the swollen red eyes of despair, the gnashing teeth of mob rage, the panicked twitchiness of fear, or the distant stare of sweet, drug-induced numbness that his calm, focused demeanor confuses the hell out of me.

"Shopping."

I pull my eyebrows together as he strides past me.

"Shopping?"

The stranger stops next to the dirt bike and shoves a black helmet onto his head, ignoring my question.

"A helmet. Really?" I snort. "We only have three days to live, and you're worried about safety regulations. You're not one of those *lifers*, are you?"

Lifer is a term the media coined months ago to describe those disgustingly optimistic members of our society who simply refused to believe that the end was near. You used to be able to tell them apart by their stupid, smiling faces and cheerful greetings. But, now, they look just like the rest of us—mad, sad, scared, or numb.

"I'm not a lifer. I just have shit to do, and it's not gonna get done if my head is splattered all over the asphalt." The boy straddles the black-and-orange machine and turns his masked face toward me. "Get on."

I consider my options. I can't exactly run back into the restaurant and ask for help. I'm in no condition to fight. I might be able to toss the painkillers in one direction and run as fast as my beat-up legs will go in the other, which could work if all he wants is the pills. But then what? Limp home and survive on pancake-syrup soup until the four horsemen of the apocalypse come to get me?

Yeah, I think I'd rather be kidnapped.

CHAPTER 2

Rain

I CLIMB ON BEHIND my captor and wrap my arms around his waist like girls do in the movies. I've never ridden a motorcycle before or a dirt bike or whatever this thing is, but I like that it gives me an excuse to hug this boy. I sigh and rest my cheek on a yellow hibiscus on the back of his Hawaiian shirt. I know it's not a real hug, but it still feels pretty damn good. I guess I haven't hugged anybody since ...

A memory gnaws at the edges of my consciousness. It must be a sad one—I can tell by the way it gets harder to breathe—so I push it back down with all the others.

If I can just keep them locked up until April 23, I won't ever have to feel them again.

The lifer stomps down on some kind of lever, and we take off like a rocket. I squeal as we round the building, holding on to him tighter with my right hand so that I can use my left to give Burger Palace the middle finger.

I smile with my cheek still pressed against his back and wonder what he smells like. All I can smell is spilled gasoline from the wrecked and abandoned cars we're weaving through at top speed. That, and the occasional overflowing dumpster.

Left, right, left, left, right.

The fluid movement and throaty roar of the engine are exhilarating and soothing, all at the same time. I want it to last forever, but a few moments later, my chauffeur slows down and turns right, pulling into the Huckabee Foods parking lot.

Somebody spray painted an F over the H on the sign so that it says *Fuckabee Foods* now, but I'm too busy freaking out to admire my handiwork.

The grocery store? No, no, no, no, no. Is this why he took me? To whore me out for food? Shit!

The parking lot is almost empty, except for a handful of motorcycles and a few delivery trucks that either got stranded or hijacked. We pull up next to a bread truck, and I feel the blood begin to pulse through my body.

I'm gonna do it. Now or never. Here we—

The second we're parked, I throw my leg over the side of the dirt bike and take off running toward the highway. At least, I thought I was going to take off running. As soon as I try, I remember that I just got the shit kicked out of me and can't manage much more than a hobble.

I get maybe ten feet away when a pair of large hands clamps down on my waist and a head of shiny brown hair appears under my arm. With one motion, the lifer stands up straight, scooping me off the ground with his shoulder in my lower back.

I scream and cling to his head with both hands as my world is turned upside down.

"No!" I shriek. "Put me down!" I thrash. "Fuck you!" I kick and pull at his hair with both hands.

The lifer suddenly bends his knees, causing his shoulder to jam into my kidney. "Fucking. Stop." He punctuates each word with a heavy breath as he struggles to keep a grasp on my flailing body.

"I'm not going in there," I pant. "You can't make me. I'd rather starve than—ugh! Ahh! Oof!"

The bastard is walking back toward the dirt bike now, and every step sends his shoulder a little deeper into my back.

He sets me on my feet between his bike and the bread truck, and then he turns me around to face him. His viselike grip has moved from my waist to my shoulders, his hair is in his face, and his eyes are narrowed in frustration.

"I need food," he spits through his clenched teeth. "They have it. And you're gonna help me get it. Now, if you will just *shut the fuck up* and listen to me, I'll make sure you get out of there with your precious little virtue intact."

I roll my eyes. "Virtue? Pssh. That shit's been gone since eighth grade."

Captain Serious completely ignores my perfectly timed joke and stares at the yellow Twenty One Pilots logo on my black hoodie. "Do you have a shirt on under that?"

"Uh ... yeah."

"Tuck it in."

I sneer at him, but the witty comeback turns to dust in my mouth as the boy strips off his Hawaiian shirt. Where I expect to see the birdcage chest and spindly arms of a teenager, I find the rippled, muscular torso of a man. A grown-ass man with actual biceps ... and tattoos on those biceps ... and abs that I can count even through his ribbed tank top.

I feel myself physically pull away from him. Guys are fun. Guys are my friends. Guys I can handle. But men ...

Men scare the shit out of me.

Especially the ones in this town.

I watch as he takes off his brown leather shoulder holster next. The gun inside must be heavy, judging by the way the veins on his arm pop out as he wraps the straps around the weapon and tucks it into the wheel well of the bread truck. Unarmed, the *man* shrugs his blue floral shirt back on, and I quickly go back to the business of shirt-tucking.

"You ready?" His eyes fall to the drawstring waistband of my plaid pajama pants, which I'm tying in a tight knot to keep my shirt in.

"No," I sass, peeking up at him through my lashes.

He rolls his eyes before tucking his disheveled brown hair behind his ears. The motion is so sweet that I almost forget about all the tattoos and muscles. He becomes a guy again.

And a guy is much easier to trust than a man.

"Just keep your mouth shut and follow my lead, okay? We're gonna be in and out."

I bite my tongue and nod, letting him guide me toward the entrance of Fuckabee Foods with a hand on the small of my back. A neckless meathead with facial tattoos is sitting in a folding lawn chair out front. He's holding an Uzi and staring at a glowing device on his lap. He's so engrossed that he doesn't look up until we're almost standing right in front of him.

"You got service?" my abductor asks, glancing at the episode of *American Chopper* playing on the guy's tablet.

"Fuck no," he snaps, furrowing his unibrow. "But I downloaded some shit before the cell towers went down." He taps the side of his head with a thick index finger. "You gotta be smart, man." The redneck who looks like he just escaped death row cuts his eyes to me and sneers, "Looks like you payin' with a *dime* today, huh?"

I have to fight back a wave of panic as his gaze slides down the length of my body.

"This?" He chuckles, giving me the side-eye. "*This*, unfortunately, is my sister. I wouldn't wish her on my worst enemy, man." He leans forward and whispers loud enough for me to hear him, "She's a biter."

I cross my arms and cock my head to one side, trying to play the part of the bratty younger sister as the ogre eyes me suspiciously.

"If you ain't sharin' the pussy, you better come correct, boy. My men ain't gonna be real happy about not gettin' a taste of that"—he licks his lips as I try not to dry-heave under his stare—"unless you got somethin' even better for 'em."

"Your men like the taste of *Hydro*?"

I don't know what the hell he's talking about until that asshole reaches into his pocket and produces an orange canister full of little white pills.

My hands fly to my stomach, squeezing and patting my now-empty hoodie pocket. "No!" I shriek, reaching out to snatch my pills back, but Human Shrek grabs them first.

With a victorious grin, he pops the cap off and shakes a handful into his mouth. "These better be real," he mumbles, crunching them to paste between his yellowed teeth. "If I ain't feeling somethin' by the time y'all leave, y'all motherfuckers is dead."

Um, you just crushed, like, five extended-release hydrocodone. I think you *might be the one who's dead, dumbass.*

Standing, he pats us down with the hand not holding the semiautomatic weapon and then hands us two plastic grocery bags from the stash hanging off the back of his chair. "Fill 'em up and get the fuck out. Twenty minutes."

As soon as the sliding glass doors close behind us, I turn and punch my captor in the stomach. "What the hell?" I hiss. "Those were mine—"

Before my temper tantrum has a chance to get started, I'm up against a wall with a hand clamped over my mouth.

"Let's get one thing straight." *Hawaii Five-O*'s pupils bore into mine like lasers, but his voice is nothing more than a whisper. "I don't *care* what *you* need. I'm here to get what *I* need. And what *I* need is food, supplies, and for you to shut the fuck up." He glances out the front door where our new friend is sitting with his back to us. "Unless, of course, you *want* homeboy's buddies to hear you. I'm sure they'd love to see the hot piece of ass he just let in here."

My eyes go wide as his palm disappears from my face. I should be upset, enraged even, but as I stare up at the grumpiest asshole I've ever met—other than my dad, of course—my stupid mouth pulls into a sideways smile.

Did he just call me hot?

My captor doesn't smile back. He simply shakes his head in a way that says, *This bitch is crazy*, and then taps an invisible watch on his exposed wrist. "Nineteen minutes. Let's go."

My smile disappears.

I hustle to keep up with him as he heads toward the center aisles. The deeper into the store we go, the louder the voices of the new occupants become and the stronger the stench of rotting food. Of course, the center aisles house all the nonperishables, which is exactly what he appears to be stocking up on. Protein bars, squeezie pouches filled with pureed fruits and vegetables, beef jerky, trail mix ...

"What's your name?" I whisper as he bends over and reaches one long arm all the way to the back of a shelf to grab the last can of beef stew. The place has been ransacked.

He looks up at me with that same flat expression. Then, he stands and drops the can into one of the bags, ignoring my question.

"You're not gonna tell me?" I whisper-pout.

Mr. Grumpy raises one eyebrow in response, then turns away from me and continues browsing the looted aisles.

"I have to call you *something*," I whisper-whine as he reads the nutrition label on a packet of ramen noodles. He puts them back. "If I guess it, will you at least nod?"

His jaw clenches, and his eyes cut to mine. "If I tell you, will you shut the fuck up?" His voice is a barely audible hiss.

I grin and nod, pretending to lock my lips shut with an invisible key.

"It's Wes."

I open my mouth to reply, then snap it shut again when his eyebrows shoot up in a silent warning.

Sorry, I mouth, holding my hands up. *I'll be quiet.*

I follow him to the cereal aisle where cornflakes and colorful, dried marshmallows crunch beneath our feet like autumn leaves, no matter how lightly we tread. As we near the end, a chorus of deep laughter bursts into the building and bounces off the rafters. *Wes* pushes me behind him and peers around the corner. Turning back to me, he places a finger to his lips, then points it in the direction of the next aisle over. The voices, too loud and rowdy to belong to sober men, travel away from us, down a path of what sounds like broken glass and sticky soda.

With tender feet, we turn left and tiptoe down aisle twelve. Hardware.

Wes stops in front of a wall of hanging tools, and I watch him with my mind occupied by two very different thoughts. Part of me can't stop thinking about his name—*Wes. I wonder what it's short for. Wesley probably. Or Wesson, like that big-ass gun he was carrying. Or maybe it's something fancy, like Westchester*—while the other part of me wonders how in the hell he's going to fit anything else into those bags. Sharp corners bulge in every direction, threatening to slice the thin plastic to shreds, yet he keeps pulling items off the wall—a flashlight, a pocketknife, a pack of lighters, and a can opener.

Then, he turns his gaze on me.

Suddenly, I know what it feels like to be a flashlight or a pocketknife or a pack of lighters or a can opener. It feels good, being looked at like that. Being chosen by this *man*. But also scary. And exhilarating. Especially when he begins walking toward me.

I hold his stare as he approaches and hold my breath when he stops right in front of me … and spreads his arms.

I don't question the invitation. I don't hesitate for a second. I step forward, wrap my arms around his waist, and rest my cheek on the hard plane of muscle above his heart. Mine thunders in my chest as I wait for his embrace, but my captor doesn't hug me back. Instead, he reaches around me, pulls the neck of my baggy sweatshirt out, and drops the packaged supplies down the back of my tucked-in tank top.

My cheeks blaze with mortification as the items slide down my bare skin, one by one.

Plunk, plunk, plunk, plunk.

God, I feel stupid.

The second the last one drops, I'm gone. I don't care about the cereal crunching under my boots or the laughing, slurring men nearby or the ogre with the Uzi waiting for us outside. All I care about is getting the fuck away from that asshole before he sees my stupid red face.

I'm almost to the exit when a trio of guys who look like they just crawled out from under a meth lab step between me and the sliding glass doors. The red bandanas showing off their redneck gang affiliation are the only colorful thing about their otherwise drab, unwashed appearances. There's a gross, predatory look in their bloodshot eyes that would send me running … if it wasn't for the handguns sticking out of their waistbands.

"What's the rush, pretty girl? You just got here."

I recognize one of them from school. He was in the grade above me, I think. At least, he was until he stopped going.

"Well, goddamn." His pale face splits into a grin, revealing a set of blackened teeth. "If it isn't little Rainbow Williams." He clicks his tongue and violates me with his cloudy eyes. "Look at you … all grown up."

I want to act cool and pal around with him like we're old friends, but I can't even remember his damn name.

I can't remember anything anymore.

I start to panic, flying through every possible name I can think of in my mind, but all I can get out is, "Hey … man."

"Looks like you and your boyfriend here"—all three guys lift their eyes to a spot over my shoulder—"were trying to leave without paying your taxes."

Taxes.

My stomach drops.

I manage to twist my face into a fake smile. "Oh! No … see, we worked it out with …" I gesture toward the doorman on the other side of the glass behind them, hoping he'll verify our payment situation, but when I glance over at him, he's not in his chair at all.

He's lying facedown on the sidewalk, being sniffed and nibbled on by a pack of wild dogs.

My guts churn as the reality of our situation comes crashing down around me. We are unarmed and outnumbered, and the only person who might have been able to help us just freaking overdosed.

I glance over my shoulder at Wes. His jaw flexes as he chews on the inside of his bottom lip. He's staring straight ahead, refusing to look at me, and I know why.

Because the lifer has something to live for.

"Can I go?" he asks in a bored voice, meeting the stares of all three gangsters as if they were obnoxious children making him late for work.

I almost want to laugh. A complete stranger took me at gunpoint and delivered me to my worst nightmare, and I let him do it because I liked the way he looked at me.

The nightmare! That's it! Any minute now, the four horsemen are going to burst through that door and kill us all! It's just the nightmare! It has to be! Wake up, Rain! Wake up!

I swing my head left and right, desperately searching for a telltale black-and-red banner, a stitch of April 23 propaganda, some flames, smoke, *something*, but the only things hanging on the walls are TV monitors showing videos of happy white people eating three-dollar bags of Doritos.

It's not a dream. It's just me, three rapists, and the guy trying to sell me to them.

Gulp.

The thugs glance at each other and then back at the man behind me.

The one on the left glares at him and spits on the ground. "Yo pussy-ass ain't even worth the bullet."

"Go on, pretty boy," the one on the right says through his gold grill, flicking his head toward the door. "Get the fuck out."

The one I recognize stares right at me, licking his thin, chapped lips. "You never said shit to me when we was in school, but now, I'm gon' have you screamin' my name."

Dread slithers through my veins as all three rotten grins close in on me, and tears sting my eyes as I watch the lifer walk right on past, leaving me to pay for his precious groceries. The sliding glass doors behind the hillbilly mafia open as my only hope strolls toward them. He stops in the doorway and gives me one last look over his shoulder. But his face isn't cold and callous, like I expected. It's not even remorseful. What I find there is sharp and direct. Wes's pupils narrow and cut to the display shelf beside him and back. Like a command.

Or a warning.

I don't have time to figure out what it means before Wes brings two fingers to his mouth and lets out the loudest whistle I've ever heard.

The dogs outside lift their heads, and before the rednecks in red even have a chance to turn all the way around, Wes grabs a bag of chips off the shelf next to him and rips the damn thing wide open. Salty orange triangles rain down on the threesome as a pack of starving dogs rushes through the open sliding doors. My brain screams at me to run, but all I can do is stand there with my mouth hanging open as the dogs overtake my attackers, snarling and yelping and gnashing and clawing at anything and everything between them and the promise of food.

As I stare at the scene before me, a hand clamps down around my wrist and drags me out the door. I don't look at the ogre on the sidewalk as we pass. I don't stop to take his machine gun or hunt for my pill bottle—two things I know I'll kick myself for later. I don't even limp. All I can think about as Wes and I run across the parking lot is getting away from that hellhole as quickly as possible.

Once we're behind the bread truck, Wes shoves the grocery bags into my arms and grabs his gun holster from the wheel well. "You okay?" he asks, shrugging the brown leather harness on over his shirt.

"Yeah," I huff, shoving my arms elbow deep into the straps of the plastic bags so that they won't fall off during the ride.

"Good." He pulls his black helmet down over his face.

Good.

My cheeks tingle as I climb onto the bike behind him. The second my ass hits the seat, I plaster myself to Wes's back, and we peel out of the parking lot and onto the highway. Shots ring out from somewhere behind us, but I don't look back.

Of course, I don't look forward either.

When you're three days away from the apocalypse, there's not much to look forward to.

CHAPTER 3

Rain

RIGHT, LEFT, RIGHT, RIGHT, *left.*

We weave back through the wreckage on the highway, and I'm lulled into a trance. The adrenaline from our escape begins to wear off—taking the last of my hydrocodone high along with it—and my mind begins to wander into dangerous places. No memories come. Just feelings. Bad ones. And the occasional unwanted picture in my head. I don't know which ones are from real life and which ones are from the nightmares.

I don't want to know.

I squeeze my eyes shut and try singing to myself, but every song that comes to mind is sad. Or violent. Or sad and violent. "Semi-Automatic" by Twenty One Pilots makes me think of "10 A.M. Automatic" by The Black Keys, which makes me think of "Black Wave" by K. Flay, which makes me think of "Blood in the Cut" by K. Flay, which makes me think of "Cut Yr Teeth" by Kississippi, which makes me think of "Cut My Lip" by Twenty One Pilots.

I begin searching for a happy Twenty One Pilots song— there has to be one—when Wes makes a sharp right, pulling into Hartwell Park. I hold on to him tighter through the turn, food bags cutting off the blood supply to my lower arms, and try to figure out what the hell we're doing there.

The place has seen better days. Burger Palace wrappers, crushed beer cans, and cigarette butts have been strewn around like confetti after a party, and in addition to all the other graffiti, *somebody* went and spray-painted a giant letter S on the sign so that it reads *Shartwell Park* now.

Okay, that one's my personal favorite.

Wes drives right up onto the grass and parks next to the playground. I let go of him, reluctantly, and climb off the dirt bike. Setting the plastic bags on the ground, I massage the divots out of my arms to try to get the blood flowing into my hands again.

As soon as his helmet is off, Wes grabs the bags and heads up a yellow ladder to the top of the playground equipment. I tilt my head back and squint up at him as he disappears over the ledge. "Why did you stop *here*? You just really like slides or something?"

"Dogs can't climb ladders," he calls back over the sound of plastic rustling and cardboard ripping.

Oh shit.

Looking around to make sure there's no sign of the three Rs, I climb up the ladder and find Wes sitting with his back against the railing, already popping the last bite of a protein bar into his mouth.

"Damn. You *were* hungry."

He wads up the wrapper and tosses it into the sea of garbage below us before offering the opened box to me. The gesture is kind, but his eyes are hard as he crunches on a cheekful of chemically engineered nutrients.

"Uh, thanks." I slide a protein bar out of the box and peel back the wrapper. The moment my teeth sink into that brick of salty sweetness, an involuntary moan rumbles in the back of my throat. It's the first thing I've eaten that hasn't come out of a deep fryer at Burger Palace in days. Maybe longer.

"That was really fucking stupid back there."

I swallow and risk a glance at my angry companion. Even though he's sitting and I'm standing, the look on his face still scares the hell out of me.

"Oh ... yeah. Sorry about that."

"I told you I'd get you out of there *if* you kept your mouth shut and followed my lead. You didn't follow shit."

I wince and manage an awkward half-smile. "I followed you, like, *almost* the whole time." My half-smile turns into a grimace.

"Yeah, and you ran your fucking mouth almost the whole time, too." Wes drops his dagger-like stare and begins rummaging through the bags again.

"I said I was sorry, okay? Maybe, next time, you should kidnap somebody a little less impulsive."

Wes rips the top off another box, ignoring me.

I cross my arms over my chest and try to pout, but it's kind of hard when he's twisting the cap off a pouch of squeezie applesauce like a five-year-old.

"Man"—I giggle—"you do *not* know how to apocalypse. We're gonna die in three days, and you're over here, worried about the five food groups."

Wes stills with the pouch poised an inch from his parted lips. "Who's *we*?"

"Um, you, me"—I spread my arms and look out over the empty landfill of a park—"everybody."

"I'm not gonna die," Wes says before wrapping his lips around the opening of the pouch.

Something about the way he's looking up at me makes my cheeks tingle.

I laugh it off and snap my fingers at him. "I knew you were a lifer! I knew it!" I sit down across from him and lean forward. "So, tell me, lifer, if we're not gonna die, what do *you* think the nightmares mean? You think the four horsemen of the apocalypse are just gonna show up on April 23 to braid our hair and play patty-cake?" At the mention of braids, I reach up and touch the place where mine used to be.

Yep. Still gone.

Wes leans forward and jams a finger in my direction. "I told you, I'm not a fucking lifer. I didn't say, *we're* not gonna die. I said, *I'm* not gonna die. I don't know what the dream means, and I don't give a shit. All I know is that whatever it is … I'm gonna survive it."

I almost choke on my protein bar. Burying my lower face in my elbow, I cough up bits of powdered peanut butter and stare at the delusional man sitting across from me. "You're gonna *survive* it?"

Wes lifts his shoulders in a half-assed shrug as the pouch between his lips flattens to nothing.

"How are you gonna survive something if you don't even know what it is?"

Another shrug. Another wrapper hits the ground.

"Been doin' it my whole life." Wes's voice is soft again, and this time, his eyes don't meet mine when he speaks.

Something inside of me twists at his admission, and I lower my voice to match his. "So, you're like, some kind of survivalist then?"

"Sure." The word comes out harsh and flat, like he doesn't want to talk about it.

That's fine with me. I'm an expert at not talking about shit. Or dealing with it at all if I don't have to.

I lean back against the railing and yelp as the items he shoved down my shirt earlier clang against the yellow metal poles. The corner of one package stabs me in the spine while the corner of another pokes me in the ass through my pajama bottoms. "Ow! God! Damn!"

With a huff, I turn around so that my back is toward him and untuck my tank top, letting all of his precious supplies fall into his lap. Wes chuckles softly, and I look at him over my shoulder.

Big mistake.

The man in the Hawaiian shirt is smiling down at the tools I just dumped on him like it's Christmas morning. His lashes are long and dark against his high cheekbones, a lock of soft brown hair has fallen out from behind his ear, and all I want to do is crawl into his lap so that maybe he'll look at me the same way.

But he won't because, unlike that flashlight, pocketknife, pack of lighters, and can opener, I'm a tool that's already served its purpose. Wes got his food, and any minute, he's going to toss me aside like all those wrappers on the ground below us.

Through the railing behind Wes, my eyes catch movement on the other side of the playground. An older couple just arrived, and they're each pushing a small child on a swing. The kids are giggling and kicking their feet, completely oblivious to the garbage and sadness all around them, but their parents' vacant, numb, washed-out stares say it all.

They're going to watch each other die in three days, and the only thing they can do about it is stay high and try not to cry in front of the kids.

I tear my eyes away from their pain, as all of mine begins to rise to the surface. Every punch and kick I took this morning makes itself known. The rejection I know is coming—when Wes announces that he doesn't need me anymore—burns like fire beneath my skin. Every loss I've suffered and the ones I know are coming pound against my skull, demanding to be acknowledged. I feel it all and all at once.

I grab my hoodie pocket, desperate for relief, but it's empty. Of course.

Because Wes stole my pills to buy these fucking groceries.

Turning back around, I shove my hands into my windblown hair and try to catch my breath, but I can't. I can't breathe. I can't get my fingers through the tangled strands.

And I can't believe I was stupid enough to let this guy take the only thing I had that would make this pain go away. I yank harder. Breathe harder. I rock back and forth, trying to soothe myself, but nothing's working.

"Hey … you okay?"

"No!" I shout, but I only hear it in my mind. My lungs are expanding and contracting—I can feel it—but the air's not getting in.

The air's not getting in!

"Rainbow …"

"Rain!" I snap, clutching the sides of my head.

"Rainbow," a sweet voice calls in my head. *"Rainbow, baby, time to come inside …"*

The image of a beautiful, smiling woman with dark blonde hair flashes behind my eyes before my flailing consciousness bats it away.

No!

"Rain …" Wes's voice is measured and calm.

He's talking to me like I'm a caged animal, so I behave like one.

I fucking run.

CHAPTER 4

Wes

"RAIN!" I SHOUT AFTER her, but she's already halfway across the parking lot.

Her limp is worse than before, but she's managing. I lean back against the railing and watch her disappear into the woods.

What the fuck was that?

I glance over my shoulder at the family she was staring at just a second ago and wonder if she knew them or something.

Whatever. It's not my problem.

My stomach growls, reminding me exactly what my problem is. Or was, before I scored a week's worth of food, thanks to that little black-haired psycho. I'm actually glad she ran off. That one had *desperate clinger with daddy issues* written all over her, and the last thing I need is another mouth to feed.

I dig through the plastic bags until I find the can of beef stew. I'm sure it'll taste like fucking dog food, but it has enough calories and protein to get me through the rest of the day.

I pick up the packaged can opener in my lap, and I swear, it fucking smells like her. Lifting the cardboard to my nose, I close my eyes and inhale, remembering the way she wrapped her little arms around me in the grocery store. Her hair smelled just like this—vanilla or cupcakes or some girlie shit. Made my dick hard.

Yeah, and then she stormed off and almost got herself gang-raped.

My heart beats like an iron fist against my ribs as I picture her standing there, watching me leave, big blue eyes full of fear, big black hoodie almost down to her knees.

Stop it. You don't need her anymore. Supplies, shelter, self-defense. That's it.

My blood pumps harder as I remember the way she tried to fight me off in the parking lot. Bitch actually pulled my hair. Nobody's ever pulled my fucking hair before.

Supplies, shelter, self-defense.

I picture the little crease in her forehead and the swelling claw marks on her cheek after I yanked her ass out of Burger Palace, standing there, debating whether or not to get on the bike with me. As if she had a choice.

Supplies, shelter, self-defense.

Then, I see her the way I found her—balled up on the floor, so tiny, taking the beating of a lifetime because she refused to hand over her precious painkillers.

Damn it!

I chuck the can back into the bag and grab my shit. My stomach protests as I leap down to the trash-covered woodchips below and begin tying the grocery bags to my handlebars with violent knots. I have to get Rain back, and it has nothing to do with the fact that she smells like sugar cookies or looks like a broken china doll dressed by a blind person or because of the way her tits and thighs felt pressed against me on the back of my bike. I have to get Rain back because I know something she doesn't.

Rainbow Williams is a fucking survivor.

And I'm not done using her yet.

I follow the trail she took through the woods on my bike, but it only leads as far as a strip shopping center down the road from the park. The place is deserted, hollowed out from a fire. If I had to guess, I'd say the looters probably took whatever drugs they could find in the dentist's office and left the rest to burn.

That's the only thing of any real value anymore. Pills. Pussy. The thrill of pyromania. Cash is worthless—unless you want to Apocasize your French fries at Burger Palace. And our government is so full of shit that nobody even listens to those lying assholes anymore. According to them, the US dollar is "stronger than ever," and we should all just "remain calm" until "the source of the nightmares is identified."

Of course, that message has been playing on a prerecorded loop for the last few weeks because not even the newscasters are showing up for work anymore. They're all at home with their families or out getting fucked up and lighting shit on fire like the rest of us.

I drive around the building and pick up the trail again, heading back the way I came. Even though I haven't been back to Franklin Springs since I was nine, I still know these woods like the back of my hand. I think I spent more time in them, avoiding my cunt of a mother and her parade of drunken boyfriends, than I ever did under her roof.

Or anyone's roof, for that matter. After I was placed in foster care, I bounced from shitty home to shittier home until I finally aged out of the whole shitty system. Now, I bounce from roommate to roommate instead.

The trail runs parallel to the main highway, stopping and restarting at almost every business along the way. A few forks jut off of it here and there, cutting through the woods to nearby neighborhoods. I'm starting to think I might have waited too long. Rain could be anywhere by now. She's probably inside some perfect little house somewhere, eating a perfect little meal, telling her perfect little family about the asshole who kidnapped her from Burger Palace.

I pop the clutch and shift into second. Then, third. I don't know if it's because I think I can still find her or if it's because I'm so fucking mad at myself for letting her go, but I tear down the trail so fast that I don't even realize where I am until the woods clear, and I find myself barreling across a huge parking lot, headed toward one very familiar-looking bread truck.

Fuck!

I hit the brakes and skid to a stop beside the truck. I listen for shots, yelling, barking, anything, but my bike is loud as fuck, so I kill the engine and wait. My gun has been a fucking paperweight ever since I used my last bullet saving Rain's ass at Burger Palace this morning, but I draw it anyway and walk my bike forward until I have a clean view of the main entrance through the driver's window.

Huckabee Foods looks exactly the way we left it—bloated corpse facedown on the sidewalk, overturned lawn chair, probably a few mauled gangbangers on the other side of the sliding glass doors. But, most importantly, no imminent threats. I breathe out a sigh of relief and holster my gun, wondering how the fuck I could be stupid enough to end up back here. I was being reckless. I don't *do* reckless.

But I know somebody who does.

Before I can crank the throttle and get the fuck out of there, something tells me to give the entrance a second look. I do, and that's when I notice that the dead guy is no longer lying on his stomach. He's rolled over onto his side. And there, squatting next to him, is the little black-haired bitch who did the rolling.

Rain's hoodie-covered body is kneeling in front of the corpse, holding one side of him up with her shoulder while she digs through the pockets of his baggy jeans. The guy's face is fucking horrifying—eyelids half-open, mouth slack, dried puke covering one side of it—but Rain is going through his shit like she's hunting through a clearance bin at Walmart.

A little fucking survivor. I knew it.

When she finds what she's looking for, Rain lets the guy's body fall back down with an unceremonious *plop*. She focuses all of her attention on something small and orange in her hands. I want to stand up and give her a slow clap for having bigger balls than I do, but I'm pretty damn sure that whatever gang produced Thug-Life Shrek and the meth-head trio, it has plenty more soldiers to spare inside.

Rain shakes a pill into her mouth. Then she caps the bottle and shoves it down the neck of her sweatshirt, tucking it into her bra. I smirk, remembering how that same bottle practically fell out of her hoodie pocket and into my hand when I threw her over my shoulder earlier.

She's learning.

Shaking my head, I stomp down on the kick-start.

Rain got what she came for. Now, it's my turn.

I pull out from behind the bread truck, expecting Rain to spin around with a smile on her face at the sound of my approaching engine.

Instead, she spins around, holding homeboy's Uzi.

It's still strapped to his massive body, but she keeps the barrel trained on me as she struggles to free it. By the time I pull up to the curb next to her, her cheeks are pink from exertion. I sit and wait with a smug smile under my helmet, knowing good and goddamn well that this girl isn't going to shoot m—

Br-r-r-r-r-ap!

The crescendo of a machine gun sounds at the exact same time that a white-hot pain slashes through my shoulder. I look to Rain in disbelief that the bitch actually pulled the trigger, but she isn't facing me anymore. She's facing the main entrance where two more of society's red bandana rejects are lying on the ground, bleeding all over a bed of broken glass.

Rain's startled eyes dart over to me before she drops the Uzi and leaps to her feet. She hesitates, then makes a mad dash for my bike, stopping to pick up one of the fallen gangbanger's pistols along the way.

Supplies, shelter, and self-defense, I recite in my head as Rain wraps her soft little body around mine.

Two down, one to go.

CHAPTER 5

Rain

I JUST KILLED A guy.

Two guys. I think I just killed two guys.

As I bounce up and down on the back of Wes's speeding dirt bike, I replay what just happened in my head. I don't *relive* it. I simply watch it, like a bad TV show, while I wait for the hydrocodone to kick in and make it all go away.

I see the reflection of the sliding glass doors opening in Wes's shiny black helmet. I see red bandanas coming out of that door. I see guns pointed at Wes. Then, I see the men holding those guns fall down as the sliding glass doors explode behind them. It looks like sparkly crystal confetti in the air. Everything is so loud. I can't believe Wes actually shot those guys. I turn back around and look at him.

But he isn't holding a gun.

I close my eyes and smoosh my cheek against Wes's shoulder blade a little harder. Then, I throw that instant replay clip into the fortress of Shit I'm Not Going to Think About Ever Again Because None of This Matters and We're All Going to Die.

Wes's body begins to twist and flex in my arms like he's trying to do something while he drives, so I sit up and peek over his shoulder. He has one hand on the handlebars while the other is messing around with his holster. I wonder if he needs my help, but before I can offer, Wes draws his gun and tosses it into the woods.

I turn my head, following the revolver with my eyes as it disappears into the underbrush. Then, I gasp as the pistol I forgot I was even holding is pulled free from my hand. Wes holsters his new gun—*my* gun—and I feel his body shake with laughter.

Asshole.

I smack him on the shoulder and hear him yelp, even over the roar of the engine.

When I look down, there's blood on my hand.

Oh my God.

Wes pulls to a stop on the side of the trail and yanks his helmet off. "What the fuck?"

"I'm sorry! I didn't know!" I slide off the leather seat and reach for the sleeve of Wes's shirt. The pink flower printed there is now bright red. "Let me look at it."

Wes glares at me and nods. Once.

He mercilessly chews on the inside of his bottom lip as I carefully pinch the edge of his sleeve. Lifting the fabric, I see a deep gash across his upper arm. It's nasty—about two inches long and half an inch wide—but not bleeding too badly. It's as if the heat from the bullet cauterized the wound.

"Well, I've got good news and bad news."

Wes raises an annoyed eyebrow at me.

"The good news is that it's just a flesh wound. The bad news is that you ruined your pretty shirt."

Wes pulls his shoulder away from me and yanks his sleeve back down. "*I* ruined it?"

"Don't look at me! The only reason those guys came outside and shot at you was because they heard *your* loud-ass bike!"

"Well, *my* loud-ass bike wouldn't have been there if *you* hadn't run away."

"Well, *you* didn't have to come get me, did you?"

Wes purses his lips and looks at me the way he would a shelf of canned goods or a rack of tools. Like he's considering my value. "Yes, I did."

He props his bike on the kickstand, and my heart begins to pound as he stands up and faces me. The vehicle is in between us, like a line in the sand.

"As much as I hate to admit it"—his face softens, just a little—"you're pretty useful when you're not trying to get us both killed."

I swallow and straighten my spine, forcing myself to look him in the eye. It's hard to act tough when you're looking at something that *pretty*. Hell, it's hard to remember what I was about to say.

Wait. What was I about to say? Oh, right.

"What makes you think I wanna help *you*?"

"What makes you think I give a shit what you want?" Poof. Softness gone.

"Gah, Wes! You don't have to be such a dick. You could just ask nicely, you know?"

Wes pulls *my* gun out of his holster and points it at my head with a smirk. "I don't have to ask nicely. I'm the one with the gun."

I roll my eyes and cross my arms over my chest.

"You know what I like about Glocks?" Wes's smirk widens into a sneer. "The safety is right here." He taps his index finger against the trigger. *Tap, tap, tap.* "You don't even have to cock the hammer back before you shoot. You just ... squeeze."

"Ugh! Fine! I'll help you!" I throw my arms in the air. "You don't have to be so dramatic about it."

Wes chuckles as he shoves the gun back into his holster. It reminds me of how he looked at the playground. Dark eyelashes fanned across his cheeks. Perfect smile. Rusty laugh. Only this time, it doesn't hurt to look at him.

Because this time, he wants me to stay.

"I need gas," Wes announces, giving his gunshot wound another quick glance. It must hurt like a bitch.

"Gas stations around here are all dry. Only way to get gas now is to siphon it."

"Cool." Wes climbs back onto the bike and looks over at me. "Know where we can find a hose?"

"And a bandage?" I glance down at the ruined sleeve of his Hawaiian shirt.

"Yeah."

"Yeah"—I swallow, trying to push the tightness out of my throat—"I do."

CHAPTER 6

Wes

Rain leads me down the trail, back through the park, and all the way to a library across from good ole Burger Palace.

"I can't believe that car is still on fire," she shouts over the growl of the engine as we pass a smoking sedan in the parking lot. "It's been burnin' all day!"

She directs me to go around to the back of the library and points to the spot in the trees where the trail continues. I head toward it but notice movement out of the corner of my eye. I turn my head and reach for my gun but relax when I see that it's just a dude … giving another dude a blow job.

"Sorry!" Rain shouts to the startled men with a giggle as we dive back into the pines.

This part of the trail isn't as well traveled, so I slow down, and for the first time all day, I don't feel like I'm running to or from anything. I suck in a deep breath, wishing I could smell the pines through my helmet, and feel Rain's warm body shuddering against mine as she continues to laugh.

Then a sapling branch whips across my mangled shoulder, and I debate burning the entire fucking forest to the ground.

"There!" Rain's finger shoots out in the direction of a clearing up ahead. "That's my house!"

Her house? This should be interesting. I'm sure her parents are gonna be real excited about their precious Rainbow bringing a gun-toting homeless guy with a weeping flesh wound home for dinner.

The trail ends in the backyard of a small wooden two-story that looks like it hasn't been painted since the South lost the Civil War. At one point, it might have been blue. Now, it's just a weathered gray, spotted with mildew and peppered with woodpecker holes.

I pull around to the front of the house and park in the driveway next to a rust-colored '90s-era Chevy pickup truck.

Any minute, I'm expecting a middle-aged guy with a beer gut and a shotgun to come bursting out the front door, chewing on tobacco and yelling at me to, *Go on now! Git!*

Maybe I should keep my helmet on a little longer ...

Rain hops off the back of my bike and runs over to a spigot on the side of the house. She cranks the handle and lifts the end of a green garden hose to her mouth. Her eyes close in ecstasy as she drinks, making me realize how thirsty I am. I don't know if I've had anything to drink all day.

I stride over and wait my turn, noticing that one side of her hair is getting wet. I want to reach out and tuck it behind her ear, but I don't. That's a boyfriend move, and the last thing I need is for this chick to get the wrong idea about us.

I don't do *us*. All *us* does is get you hurt or killed, so I throw an E on the end of that bitch, and I *use*.

My foster parents used me to get money from the state. I used them to get food, water, and shelter. The girls at school used me to fill their needy little attention buckets and make each other jealous. I used them as a nice warm place to put my dick. The guys used me to score them drugs or guns or cool points or the answers to next week's history exam. I charged them a shitload to do it. This is the way the world works, and watching Rain clutching that hose in her fist—sucking from the stream with her little pink tongue at the edge of her slightly open mouth—makes me think of a few new ways I could use her, too.

As if she could hear my inappropriate thoughts, Rain lifts her big blue eyes to mine.

I smirk down at her. "There something wrong with your sinks?"

Rain jerks the hose away from her mouth and coughs.

"You okay?"

"Yeah, I just ..." She hacks some more, wiping her mouth on the back of her sleeve. "I lost my keys, remember? I can't get in."

"Whose truck is that? Can't they let you in?" I jerk my thumb in the direction of the rust bucket on wheels.

"That's my dad's, but ..." Her face goes white as her eyes dart left and right, looking for a lie. "He's deaf. *And* he hangs out in his man cave upstairs all day, so he won't hear me knocking."

"Or see you knocking," I add.

"Right." Rain shrugs dramatically.

"Where's your mom?" I take the hose from her and drink while I wait for her to make up another bullshit story.

"She's at work."

I take a breath between gulps. "Nobody's at work."

"No, for real!" The pitch of her voice shoots up along with her eyebrows. "She's an ER nurse. The hospital is still open."

I give her a doubtful glare. "How does she get there?"

"Motorcycle."

"What kind of motorcycle?"

Rain's face reddens. "I don't know! A black one!"

I laugh and shut off the water. There are a dozen smart-ass responses on the tip of my tongue, but I decide to keep my mouth shut. If this girl doesn't want me to know that she lives alone—which is pretty fucking obvious from her bullshit responses—then that's what I'm gonna let her think.

Besides, I can't say that I blame her. I'm sure *Invite a strange man into your house after he pulls a gun on you* is in the top ten list of shit single girls are taught not to do.

Invite a strange man into your house after he pulls a gun on you twice is probably in the top five.

Rain turns her flustered head toward the Chevy. "You can siphon the gas out of my dad's truck since the roads are too trashed to drive it anyway. I guess just use the"—her eyes dart back to me as I flick open my new pocketknife and slice off about five feet of hose—"hose."

"Thanks." I smirk. Walking over to the rust bucket, I cut the length of hose in my hand into two pieces—a long one and a short one. Then, I pop open the gas cap and stick both inside the opening. "Hold these, okay?"

Rain hops over like her ass is on fire. I find it interesting that she's completely incapable of following directions unless I'm asking her for help.

She probably would have been a nurse, like her mom, I think. *If her mom even is a nurse.*

I pull off my holster, making sure not to graze my shoulder wound with it, and set it on the ground. I see the way Rain is eyeing it, so I push it further away with my foot. "Uh-uh-uh."

"That's *my* gun." Rain pretends to pout as I take off my Hawaiian shirt and stuff it into the openings around the hoses.

I move her hands so that she's holding the shirt and the hoses in place.

"Can't you just, like, stick a tube in there and suck on it?" Rain asks as I walk my bike closer to the truck.

"Sure, if I wanted to get a mouthful of gasoline."

Rain rolls her eyes, and the expression makes her seem so young. That giant Twenty One Pilots hoodie doesn't help.

"How old are you?" I ask, tilting my bike sideways so that the gas tank will be lower than the truck's.

"Nineteen."

Bullshit.

"How old are you?" she asks as I stick the end of the long hose into my gas tank.

"Twenty-two."

Keeping my bike tilted at just the right angle, I lean over to where Rain is holding everything in place and blow into the short tube. She gasps a moment later when we hear the sound of liquid splashing against the bottom of my gas tank.

"Where did you learn how to do that?" Rain's eyes are wide, her voice is breathy, and her mouth has fallen open in a little O.

I begin to think of a few other ways I could put that look on her face when I remember that she asked me a question. "YouTube."

"Oh, right." She laughs. "The internet's been down for a week, and I already forgot about YouTube."

An awkward silence stretches between us as we're forced to stand there, each holding our own end of the hose.

Rain breaks it and manages to make things even more awkward. "I can't believe we only have three days left."

"Speak for yourself," I snap.

"Oh, right." Rain furrows her brow, considering my statement. "Hey, can I ask you a question?"

I shrug. "You're going to anyway."

"If whatever's coming is as bad as everyone thinks it is, then why are you trying so hard to survive it? I mean, what if you end up being the last person on Earth?"

"Then, I'd be king of the fucking world," I deadpan. The tank is almost full, so I stand the bike upright to stop the flow.

Rain lets out a sad laugh as I pull out the hose and screw the gas cap back on. "Yeah, you'd be king of the whole busted, ruined planet."

I shrug and push the kickstand back out. I never talk about my shit, but there's something about the way this girl is hanging on my every word that makes them just start falling out of my mouth. "The way I see it, if I can survive the fucking apocalypse, then it makes everything I've been through mean something, you know? Like, instead of breaking me … they made me unbreakable."

Rain's big, sad eyes begin to glisten, making me wish I'd kept my fucking mouth shut. I don't want her pity. I want her compliance. I want her resources. And, if I'm being honest, I wouldn't mind bending her over the hood of this truck right now either.

"Who is *they*?" she asks as I pull her death grip off the hoses and toss them into the overgrown grass.

"Doesn't matter." I pick my holster up off the ground and carefully pull it back on over my wifebeater. "All that matters is that, if I'm still here and they're not, then I won."

"Well, whoever they are"—Rain gives me a small smile as I fan my shirt in the air to smooth out the wrinkles—"I hope they die last."

A laugh bursts out of me as I look at Rain's angelic face. She starts laughing too, then snatches my lucky shirt out of my hands.

"Oh my God, were you seriously about to put this back on?" She cackles. I grab my shirt and try to pull it out of her hands, but she clings to it with dear life. "How are you gonna survive the apocalypse wearing a shirt soaked in gasoline?"

"I don't exactly see any laundromats around here, do you?" I fake left and grab the shirt when she veers right, but she still doesn't let go.

"I can wash it."

"What? When your mom gets home from work and lets you in?"

Rain's face pales, and she releases my shirt.

Fuck. I didn't mean to call her out.

"Yeah," she says, her eyes losing focus and dropping to my chest, "when my mom gets home."

Shit. Now, she looks all sad and freaked out. Her hand is in her hair again. That's never good. This bitch does stupid shit when she's freaking out.

"Hey," I say, trying to snap her out of it. "You wanna eat?" I drape my shirt over my good shoulder and begin untying the grocery bags hanging from my handlebars. "I saw a tree house in your backyard. We should eat up there—"

"In case the dogs smell the food," Rain finishes my sentence with a faraway look on her face.

"No." I grin, holding the bags with my good arm and guiding her into the almost-knee-high grass with my other. "Because it's probably full of Justin Bieber posters. He's so fucking dreamy."

Rain snorts through her nose like a pig. "Oh my God." She cackles. "Did you just make a joke?"

I raise an eyebrow at her and keep walking. "I would never joke about the Biebs."

As Rain falls into step beside me, snickering at my stupid fucking joke, I realize that I might have been wrong earlier.

I already feel like the king of the world.

CHAPTER 7

Rain

I SHOVE ALL THE thoughts of my mother back into the Shit I'm Never Going to Think About Again Because None of This Matters and We're All Going to Die fortress, pull up the drawbridge, and light that bitch on fire.

Three more days.

As I climb the ladder to my rickety old tree house, I realize that it's already starting to get dark outside.

Make that two and a half more days.

All I have to do is not think about her for two and a half more days, and then I won't have to think about her ever again.

I pop another pill while I wait for Wes to climb the ladder, just to make extra sure that shit stays locked up tight.

I take the bags from him as he climbs over the top of the ladder.

The tree house isn't much. It's basically just a rotting plywood box with a couple of dirty-ass beanbag chairs and an old boom box inside, but when I was a kid, it was Cinderella's castle, Jack Sparrow's pirate ship, and Wonder Woman's invisible plane, all rolled into one.

The ceiling is so low that Wes doesn't even bother trying to stand up. He simply crawls over to a beanbag chair and makes himself at home. He stretches his long legs out in front of him and crosses them at the ankles as he rummages through the grocery bags. His feet almost stick out the door. It reminds me of Alice in Wonderland when she grew too fast and got stuck in the White Rabbit's house.

"So," I say, plopping into the beanbag next to him as he concentrates on working that damn can opener that stabbed me in the back earlier, "you got anything in there that *doesn't* look like dog food?"

Wes hands me one of the bags without looking up.

I pull out a stick of beef jerky and gesture toward the clunky radio with it. "Hey, do you want to listen to some music? I think I have my mom's old Tupac CD in here. It's not *Justin Bieber*, but …"

Wes smirks at my joke and pops a chunk of potato into his mouth. "Save your batteries. We won't have power much longer."

His statement wipes the smile right off my face.

Oh, right. Apocalypse. Yay.

I take in Wes's dirty clothes as he starts pulling chunks of beef, carrots, and potatoes out of the can with his fingers like a starved raccoon. His messy hair. His total lack of personal belongings.

"So …" I pretend to look for a way to open the jerky package. "Where did you come from?"

"Here," Wes says between bites.

I laugh. "You are *so* not from here. I've lived here my whole life, and I've never seen you before."

Wes gives me a look that says he does not appreciate being called a liar, then deadpans, "I lived here until I was nine. Then, I ... moved around a lot."

"Really? Do you still have family here?"

Wes shrugs and returns to his canned dinner.

"You don't know? Who are you staying with?" I still haven't touched my jerky.

Why am I so nervous to talk to this guy? He's just a guy. Of manly age and stature. Okay, he's a fucking *man* and I don't know him and he has a gun and he's currently my only source of food that isn't a condiment.

"You."

Wait. What?

"Ohhh no. You can't stay with me. Are you fucking kidding? My parents would—"

"Not in there." Wes gestures toward my house with a cube of beef pinched between his thumb and index finger. Then, he tosses it into his mouth and points toward the floor. "Out here."

"Oh." I relax a teensy, tiny bit. "I guess that's okay."

"I wasn't asking," Wes mumbles as he chews, plucking a carrot out of his can next.

"Where are your parents?" I ask, still trying to put all the pieces together.

Wes tosses back the wet orange vegetable. "I never met my dad, and my mom's locked up."

"Oh, damn. I'm sorry."

"Don't be. She deserves worse." Wes's voice is emotionless as he selects a potato.

"Uh ... brothers or sisters?"

His annoyed eyes cut to mine but only for a second before he returns to his meal. "No."

"Then, why—"

Wes's head snaps up. "I came back because I found a bomb shelter here when I was a kid. Okay? Out in the woods." He takes a deep breath through his nose and releases it. When he continues, his voice is a little less defensive. "My plan was to find it this afternoon, after I got supplies … but I burned all my daylight looking for your ass instead."

Wes and I both look out the door at the same time. A dark blue has fallen over the sky, covering our sunset and tucking it in for the night. That's what Wes's comment feels like. I know he meant it to be a jab, but it landed on me like a blanket.

Wes chose finding *me* over finding shelter for the night.

I stare at his profile as his gaze returns to the can he's holding. I want to reach out and run my finger down the bridge of his perfect nose. I want to trace the edge of his strong jaw and feel the sandpaper scratchiness of his evening stubble against my fingertip. I want to press that finger between his full pink lips and let him bite it off if he wants to.

Because if Wes thinks he needs me, I'm determined to prove him right.

A chill racks my body as the last of the sun's warmth disappears along with the color from the sky. "I'll be right back," I say, chucking the beef jerky and trail mix back into one of the bags and scrambling over to the ladder.

Wes doesn't question where I'm going, but his gaze is a silent warning. If I try to run again, he'll find me.

I try not to smile about that until I'm halfway down the ladder.

CHAPTER 8

W es

GREAT JOB, ASSHOLE. YOU *made her fucking run again.*

Look, there she goes.

I sit up and watch Rain's hoodie-shrouded silhouette sprint across the backyard and disappear around the side of the house like she can't get away from me fast enough.

Maybe she just needs to pee.

Well, if she's not back in sixty fucking seconds, I'm going after her.

About thirty-five seconds later, I hear a loud crash, like the sound of a window breaking. I lurch forward, ready to jump out of that fucking tree house and see what the hell is going on, but before I make it to the ladder, I see a light come on inside the house. Followed by another one, and another one. I shake my head and flop back down in my seat.

That bitch just broke into her own damn house.

I toss a handful of trail mix into my mouth and watch as lights go on and off in various rooms.

What the hell is she doing in there?

It's pitch-black outside now, so I dig the flashlight out of one of the grocery bags and turn it on, setting it down so that it shines at the opposite wall. It illuminates a pack of cigarettes sticking out of a crack between the floorboard and wall.

Fuck yeah.

I dig them out—Marlboro Reds—and flip open the lid. When I turn the box over to shake one out, nothing but tobacco dust pours into my hand.

Goddamn it.

I throw the box into the corner and hear the sound of a door slamming in the distance. Seconds later, Rain is full-on sprinting across the lawn with her arms full of God knows what. The house is dark again.

Rain grunts as she climbs the ladder with her arms full, but instead of her head emerging first, a bundle of blankets and pillows comes flying over the threshold before her. Then, a tiny hand setting a bottle of whiskey down on the plywood floor with a thud, followed by the face and body of the girl it belongs to.

Rain is wearing a backpack that's almost as big as she is. She shrugs it off her shoulders and sits cross-legged next to it in the middle of the floor. Tearing it open, Rain begins talking a mile a minute.

"So, I got you some blankets and a towel and a pillow, and I filled up a couple of water bottles in case you get thirsty. Oh, and I got you some toilet paper and an extra toothbrush and all these little travel-sized toiletries from the one time my parents took me to the beach. We stayed at a real hotel that time, not just a friend of my dad's that he told me to call *Uncle This* or *Uncle That,* like all our other 'vacations.'" She put finger quotes around the word *vacations* and continues unpacking. "I remember I tried to order fried chicken from the hotel restaurant, and a lady in the back started screaming, 'Fried chicken? Fried chicken!' And then she stormed out the front door and threw her apron on the floor next to my booth on her way out. When our waiter came back, he said, 'Welp, the cook just quit. How 'bout some grilled cheese?'"

Rain cackles at the memory. The sound is manic. Pressured.

"I would have gotten you some warmer clothes too, but mine won't fit you and my dad's are in his room and"—she goes back to digging in the backpack even though it's empty now, her left knee bouncing so hard and so fast that it begins to shake the tree house—"I don't wanna go in there."

Abandoning the backpack, Rain grabs the bottle of Jack Daniel's and takes a swig, wincing and hissing in agony as it goes down. Then, another. And another.

"Hey"—I reach over and pull the bottle from her hand, and she releases it without a fight—"you okay?"

"I'm fine!" She cuts her eyes away and shoves her hands into her hair.

I know she's a pill head, but Hydro doesn't do *this*. Whatever *this* is, it happened inside that house.

Now she's rocking back and forth again.

Awesome.

"Rain."

Her eyes lift to mine, partially illuminated from my flashlight, and there's a wild desperation in them that makes me realize I read this entire situation wrong.

Rain doesn't live alone.

Rain lives with a fucking monster.

"You're scared of him, aren't you?"

"Who? I'm not scared." Rain glances over at the house as if he can hear her, knee bouncing, breaths shallow.

"Yes, you are. Look at you."

She swallows and looks down at her knee. As she stills her leg, Rain's chin buckles and begins to wobble instead.

My teeth clench so hard I feel like they might shatter. Jerking my chin toward the house, I manage to grind out, "That motherfucker hurt you?"

She claps her hands, completely covered by her hoodie sleeves, over her mouth and nose. Then, she closes her eyes and shakes her head. I can't tell if she's answering my question or trying to rid herself of some unwanted memory, but I don't care.

"Stay out here tonight."

Rain opens her eyes but doesn't take her hands away from her face.

"Let me rephrase that." I sit up and jam my finger into the plywood floor. "You're staying out here tonight."

When Rain doesn't argue, I lean back and take a long pull from the bottle in my hand.

Damn, that's good.

I toss the bag of trail mix into her lap. "Eat. I got shit to do tomorrow, and you're gonna be worthless if you're starving."

"You want me to come?" Rain mumbles into her hands.

Even with her face partially covered and the only light in the tree house coming from a pocket flashlight aimed at the wall, I can see the hope in her big blue eyes.

Fuck. Why did I say that? I don't need her anymore.

Because she's useful, I tell myself. *She's a resource—that's all— and she's the best one you've got.*

I tip the neck of my bottle at her. "You can come—as long as you promise not to eat all the fucking M&M's outta there."

Rain lowers her hands, revealing a smile that she's trying to hide by biting her lip, and uses them to dig through the bag of trail mix in her lap. Pulling her hand out, she holds up one perfectly round piece of red candy between her fingers. Then, she fucking flicks it at me. It's so dark on my side of the tree house that I can't see where it went, but I hear it bounce off the plywood wall somewhere to my right.

"Bitch." I chuckle, taking another swig of whiskey.

That little comment earns me two more M&M's to the head.

"Oh, it's on now!" I grab the stick of beef jerky and lunge forward, swatting her with it until she's nothing but a giggling, hoodie-covered heap on the plywood floor. Then, I sit back, smug in my victory, and survey my spoils for the day.

Supplies? Check.

Shelter? Check.

Self-defense? Check.

Slightly psychotic teenager with a pill habit, daddy issues, and impulse control problems?

I smirk at the hiccupping heap of girl in the fetal position across from me.

Jackpot.

CHAPTER 9

Wes

I TAKE A DEEP breath and exhale as I shift into second gear. I don't even care that I probably just sucked up two lungfuls of pollen. The woods here have been calling me home ever since I left thirteen years ago. Everything is just the way I remember, except greener. Taller. And, now that I'm exploring them on a Yamaha instead of some busted, old thrift-store sneakers ... faster.

We managed to shove all the food and supplies into Rain's backpack, but since there was no way she could wear that big-ass thing and not fall off the back of my bike, I decided to wear it and let her sit in front of me.

Worst. Decision. Ever.

Rain's ass rubbing against my dick is making it fucking impossible to keep my raging hard-on down. I've tried thinking about politics. About baseball. About Will Ferrell's naked, hairy ball sack. But nothing's working. My mind keeps going back to how easy it would be to just pull those little pajama bottoms down and let Rain bounce on my dick for real.

We drive over a patch of tree roots in the path, and I swear to God, that bitch arches her back and presses against me even harder through the bumps.

I can't fucking take it anymore.

"Throttle," I growl into her ear as I release the right handlebar.

We slow down for just a second before Rain grabs the handle. She twists the shit out of it, and we shoot forward. I laugh as she dials it back and can feel how hard she's breathing where her back meets my chest. I have to keep the clutch engaged with my left hand, but now, my right hand is free to do something about the evil little tease sitting in my lap.

Wrapping my arm around her waist, I tuck my nose into the neck of her hoodie and inhale the warm, sugary scent coming off of her heated skin. Rain's heavy breaths all but stop. Then, she angles her head to the side, just a little.

It's all the invitation I need. She keeps her eyes on the path and steers us with jerky movements as my tongue forges a trail of its own up her neck.

Fuck. She even tastes like vanilla.

I slide my hand up her body until it's filled with the weight of her perfect, round tit. Then, I smile because I can tell how hard her nipple is, even through her sweatshirt. I circle it with my thumb and feel her moan vibrate against my chest.

She can't even hide how badly she wants this, and thank fuck for that because, with my cock pressed against her ass, neither can I.

I trace the outline of her ear with my tongue as I work her other nipple, squeezing and kneading and wishing like hell that I could flip her around, yank that hoodie up, and suck it between my teeth.

I glance up just to make sure Rain isn't about to drive us off a cliff. Then, I slide my hand lower and push my fingers beneath the loose drawstring waistband of her soft flannel pajama pants. They skate over a silky pair of panties. I cup her pussy and bite her earlobe, waiting for her to tell me to stop, to swat my hand away.

But she doesn't. Instead, Rain reaches behind her back with her free hand and grabs my dick through my jeans.

Fuck.

Yes.

I'm determined to drive her just as crazy as she's been driving me this entire ride, so I rub two fingers from her clit to her hole in slow, gentle strokes, over *her panties. But Rain's impulsive ass manages to unbutton my fly and get my zipper down in seconds. The moment her smooth fingers wrap around my cock, my plan to tease her mercilessly goes right out the window. It feels so fucking good that I yank her panties aside and slide two fingers into her slick, hot pussy.*

Rain's head falls back to my shoulder, so I look up and try to concentrate on the trail while she whimpers and fucks my hand.

But we aren't on the trail anymore. At least, not any trail I've ever been on.

This one cuts through a forest of dead trees that are in the process of being consumed by sharp, thorny vines. The taller branches, brittle and gray and bent toward the white sky, have red banners hanging from them. We're going so fast that I can't read what any of them say, but I can tell that each one is branded with the silhouette of a hooded figure on horseback.

The vines reach up from the forest floor like octopus tentacles, winding around the ancient trees and squeezing them until the wood splinters and breaks and crumbles into the ocean of hungry thorns.

"Faster!" I yell to Rain, but she doesn't crank the throttle.

She begins pumping my dick even harder instead.

Fuck, it feels good.

I shove my fingers into her deeper and rub her clit with my thumb and thrust into her hand even though I know that if I don't kick it into third gear right fucking now, we're both going to die.

I can hear myself yelling inside my own head.

What the fuck are you doing?

I can see myself, a slave to my stupid desire for this crazy girl.

She's going to get you killed, dipshit! Ditch the bitch and get the fuck out of here!

But I'm powerless. Rain is in control now, and she's driving us straight toward certain death.

A tree snaps up ahead, and the sound echoes through the woods like a gunshot. As it crashes to the ground, one of its branches falls across the trail. I can clearly see the banner attached to it now, waving like a flag on the way down.

Just above the image of a faceless horseman wielding a flaming club is the date April 23.

I don't have time to contemplate what that means because, a split second later, I'm flying over the handlebars and somersaulting down the rocky, root-covered trail. When I finally stop rolling, I smack my head on something hard. My cranium explodes in pain. I sit up, clutching my dented skull, and begin frantically looking around for Rain. Blood trickles down my arm as I swivel toward the sound of cavalry in the distance.

Four monstrous black horses are barreling toward me through the forest—heads down, smoke pouring from their flared nostrils—ripping through the brambles and branches like party streamers. They leave nothing but flames and scorched earth in their wake as their faceless, cloaked riders point their weapons—a sword, a scythe, a mace, and a flaming club—toward the colorless sky.

"Wes!" Rain's voice calls out.

I swing my dented head left and right, but I don't find her until I turn all the way around. She landed in a thicket of thorn bushes, and all I can see is her face and halo of black hair before the vines constrict around her body and pull her under.

"Wesssss!"

"No!" I run toward her, but the vines grab my legs, their thorns digging into my clothes and skin like fish hooks, and pull me down, too.

Trees pop and hiss and collapse all around me as the heat from the approaching fire intensifies. I struggle to free myself, slicing my hands open as I rip the sharp vines from my body. With every push and pull and grunt and shove, I get closer to the place where Rain disappeared.

My vision is blurry and red. My head feels like it's about to implode. My hands are shredded and almost worthless, but with one last thrash, I make it out. I stumble toward the spot where I last saw Rain, calling her name with every labored step, but when I get there, she's gone.

Leaving nothing behind but a puddle of water.

I peer into it—exhausted, confused, desperate—but all I find is my own frantic, bloodied reflection staring back at me.

Then the image splashes away, stomped out by one giant black hoof.

CHAPTER 10

April 21
Rain

"WES. WES, WAKE UP. It's just the nightmare. You're okay. You're here."

Wes is sleeping sitting up. His good shoulder and the side of his head are leaning against the wall of the tree house, and he has my old comforter pulled up to his chin. He yelled my name so loud in his sleep that it woke me up. Luckily, I hadn't been asleep long, so my horsemen hadn't shown up yet, but from the looks of things, Wes's are on the other side of his eyelids right now. His entire face is tensed up, as if he's in pain, and he's breathing hard through his nose.

"Wes!" I want to shake him, but I'm afraid to touch his shoulder. I bandaged it up before we went to sleep last night, and it was pretty gross. I decide to squeeze his thighs and shake his legs instead. "Wes! Wake up!"

His eyelids flash open. They're alert and alarmed, and they land on me like a laser scope.

I hold my hands up. "Hey! You're okay. It was just the nightmare. You're safe."

Wes blinks. His eyes dart all over the tree house, out the door behind me, and then land back on mine. He's still breathing heavy, but his jaw relaxes a little.

"You're okay," I repeat.

Wes takes a deep breath and scrubs a hand down his face. "Fuck. What time is it?"

"I don't know. I stopped carrying my phone when the cell towers went down." I look out the door and notice a faint orange haze where the treetops meet the sky. "Maybe six thirty? The sun's coming up."

Wes nods and sits up, rubbing the side of his head where it was pressed against the wall all night.

"That was a bad one, huh?" I ask, taking in his battle-worn appearance.

He stretches as much as he can in the confined space and gives me a sleepy-eyed stare. "Not all of it."

Something in his tone of voice or maybe the look in his eye makes my cheeks flush. "Oh. Uh, that's good." I turn and begin rummaging through the backpack, trying to hide my blush.

"Did you fix your hair?" I don't look up, but I can feel his eyes on me. "It's all shiny."

"Oh." I laugh. "Yeah. I woke up when I heard my mom get home last night, so I went inside to say hey. I figured, while I was in there, I might as well take a shower, brush my teeth, change my clothes ..." My voice trails off when I realize that I'm rambling. I look down at the skinny jeans and hiking boots sticking out from under my hoodie as a prickly heat begins to crawl up my neck. I wanted something that was cute but woodsy. You know, *bomb-shelter chic*. Now, I'm wishing I'd just put a bag over my head.

Wes leans forward and peeks around my hair, which I straightened with a flat iron and evened out with a pair of scissors after the jagged braid-ectomy I gave myself the other night.

"Are you wearing *makeup*?"

"Yeah! So?"

Oh my God, I'm yelling.

"You just look … different."

"Whatever." I grab the travel-sized toiletry kit and the towel out of the backpack and shove them into his chest. "*You* can go take a shower with the hose."

"Damn." Wes chuckles. "That's cold."

"Literally." I grin. "Go on. I wouldn't want you to lose your precious *daylight*." I throw his words from last night back in his face as he crawls past me toward the door.

"You're not coming?"

"To watch you wash yourself? No, thanks." I roll my eyes and do my best to pretend like his perfectly chiseled abs disgust me.

"That's good 'cause there's gonna be some serious shrinkage."

I laugh as Wes climbs down the ladder. Then, I remember something. As soon as he gets to the bottom, I lean out the doorway and drop his Hawaiian shirt onto his face.

Wes pulls the royal-blue fabric off his head and holds it to his nose. "Holy shit. You washed it?"

"Yeah. It smells better now, but that blood is never coming out."

The smile that beams back up at me makes my body tingle all over.

"Thanks." Wes drapes the shirt over one shoulder and gives me a wicked side-eye. "You sure you don't wanna come wash my back?"

"Ha! And see your *shrinkage*? I'll pass."

Wes shrugs with a sideways smile and walks across the yard toward the side of the house. The second he's out of sight, I let out the breath I was holding and shove my hand up inside my hoodie. Grabbing the bottle of hydrocodone I stashed in my bra, I pull it out and shake a little white pill into my hand. I toss it back with a sip from one of the water bottles and realize that the liquid inside is sloshing like crazy, thanks to my trembling hand.

Better make that two.

CHAPTER 11

Wes

I DON'T CARE HOW heavy that backpack is; after the dream I had this morning, Rain's ass is wearing it, *and* she's sitting on the back.

I shove my helmet on over my towel-dried hair but pause before kick-starting the bike. I'm afraid the sound of the engine will cause Rain's shithead of a father to come running out, guns blazing, but maybe she was telling the truth about him being deaf after all.

Maybe she was telling the truth about her mom, too.

I look around for her mom's fabled motorcycle—the "black one"—but there's no sight of it. I guess she could have parked in the garage, but from the looks of this place, that door probably doesn't even work anymore.

I pull my helmet off and turn to Rain, who is struggling to climb on behind me with that big-ass pack on. "What did your mom say about the dirt bike in the driveway?"

"Huh?" she asks, swinging her leg over the seat with a grunt.

"Your mom? Did she ask about my bike? She would have had to drive around it to get into the garage."

"Oh. Right." Rain wraps her arms around my ribs as tight as she can to keep from falling backward. "I told her I was letting a friend stay in the tree house."

I can't tell if she's lying or not. She sounds convincing, but her eyes look a little extra crazy. Maybe it's just all that mascara. I fucking hate it. I don't need Rain to get hotter. I need her to get uglier so that I can fucking focus on surviving the next two days.

"Don't you need to go inside and tell her bye?"

"No. She's sleeping."

"And your dad?"

"Passed out in his chair."

"Well, shouldn't you, like, leave a note telling her where you're going or something?"

Rain cocks her head to the side and raises her eyebrows. "Wes, I'm nineteen years old."

I shrug. "I don't know how this family shit works, okay?"

She sighs and drops the attitude. It only lasts a second, but in that moment, I see the real Rain. Underneath all those fake smiles and that sassy attitude is a black ocean of sadness crashing against a crumbling lighthouse of hope.

"Neither do I," she admits. Then, she presses her cheek to my shoulder.

Fuck me.

I stomp down on the kick-start and head through the backyard, realizing that my dream this morning wasn't just a nightmare; it was a premonition.

The way Rain's body feels wrapped around mine, the way she looks, all dolled up like we're going on a fucking date, the way she wants to help me even though nobody's fucking helping her, I'm distracted by it. All of it. This bitch is going to get into my head, make me veer off course, and get us both killed. I know it like I know my own name, yet here we go anyway, into the woods.

CHAPTER 12

Rain

WE'VE BEEN OUT HERE for hours. The morning chill is long gone. Now, it's just hot and humid and hazy as hell, thanks to the pollen bomb that seems to have gone off somewhere nearby. Maybe that's why these people built a bomb shelter. It wasn't to protect them from nuclear fallout. It was to protect them from breathing all this crap in the air.

Wes is so serious about finding this place. *So* serious. Last night and this morning, he actually joked around with me a little bit, but ever since we left the house, he's been all business. I feel like I can't get a good read on him. Sometimes, he's relaxed and funny and ... I don't know ... kind of flirty? Then, other times, he looks at me like he hates me. Like I'm his annoying little sister, and he's sick of me tagging along.

Maybe it's because I'm not being very helpful right now. He's nicer when I'm helping him.

All I'm doing is walking around, poking the ground with a big stick.

Wes said the bomb shelter was underground, and the only entrance was a metal door, like a big, square manhole on the ground. It must have been built in the '60s, back when family fallout shelters were all the rage, but by the time Wes found it, the only thing left of the house it belonged to was a crumbling stone chimney.

We've been looking for that damn chimney all morning. I don't have the heart to tell Wes that I've spent my whole life in these woods and have *never* seen an old stone chimney, but I guess it's possible that it fell over after he left. A lot can happen in thirteen years.

Hell, here lately, a lot can happen in thirteen minutes.

"Are you *sure* it was behind Burger Palace?" I ask in a teensy, tiny voice.

We've poked every square foot of earth back here, and that door is either buried so deep in pine needles that a stick isn't gonna do the trick or we're in the wrong place.

"Yes, I'm fucking sure. I lived right down there," Wes growls, shoving his finger in the opposite direction of the highway. "I used to walk by that goddamn chimney every day on my way to ..." His voice trails off and he shakes his head, trying to get rid of the memory. "Ugh!" Wes drops the backpack on the ground and sits next to it on a fallen tree trunk, pressing his fingertips into his forehead. His freshly washed hair falls over his face, curling at the ends where it was tucked behind his ear.

I take a seat a few feet down from him on the log and unzip the pack, pretending to look for a bottle of water or something. "Sorry we haven't found it yet. I'm sure we're close. Some stupid kid probably knocked the chimney down or something."

Wes doesn't even look at me.

You're making it worse. Just shut up.

I see the bag of trail mix, so I pull it out and extend it toward Wes. "M&M?" I smile, giving the bag a little shake.

Wes turns his head toward me—one eye hidden behind that curtain of hair—and gives me an almost smile. It's just a twitch at the corner of his mouth really, and I can't tell if it's a *thanks, but no thanks* kind of twitch or the *I'm glad you're here* kind or the dreaded *you're annoying the shit out of me, and I'm just tolerating you until I can figure out how to get rid of you* kind. Before I realize what I'm doing, I reach out with my free hand and tuck that hair back behind Wes's ear so I can get a better look at his confusing expression.

Which makes his almost smile disappear completely.

Shit.

Wes is now giving me the same look he gave me behind Burger Palace yesterday. The one that freezes the air in my lungs. The one that is focused and emotionless and intimidating as hell. I wonder what he's thinking about when he looks at me like that. What he's hiding.

I realize that I'm staring at him with my hand poised awkwardly in midair behind his ear, so I drop my eyes and yank my arm back. "We're gonna find it," I blurt out, unable to think of anything else to say.

"Yeah? And what if we don't?"

I peek back up at him from under my mascara-coated lashes. "We die?"

Wes nods real slow and chews on the corner of his mouth as he studies me. "Why do I get the feeling that you're not too upset about that?"

Because I'm not.

Because I'm looking forward to it.

Because I'm too chickenshit to do it myself.

I shrug and settle on, "Because it means I get a do-over."

"No, it doesn't," Wes snaps, sitting up straighter. "It means you *are* over. Don't you get that? It means you lost, and they won."

I want to tell him that I'm okay with that, whoever "they" are, but I know it'll only lead to more questions. Questions I don't want to answer. Questions that will rattle the locks on Fort Shit I'm Not Going to Think About Ever Again Because None of This Matters and We're All Going to Die. So, I keep my mouth—and the drawbridge—shut tight.

Besides, if Wes knows I'm just using him as a distraction, that I don't actually *want* to survive whatever the hell is coming for us, he might not let me tag along anymore. And tagging along with this asshole is kinda my only reason for living at the moment.

I sigh and look around the woods, praying for a burst of inspiration that will help me convince him that we're in this together.

Blowing out a breath, I lean forward and place my elbows on my knees. "If only we had a metal detector or something."

"That's it!" Wes snaps his fingers and points at me in the same motion.

I glance over at him and give myself an internal high five when I see his beautiful, megawatt smile beaming back at me.

"That's fucking it! Rain, you're a goddamn genius!" Wes stands up and ruffles my hair before lifting the backpack off the ground and holding the straps open for me to slip into. "Where's the closest hardware store?"

I push my messed up hair out of my face and point toward the highway.

"Let's go!"

"Okay, okay," I grumble, standing up and turning around so that he can drop that fifty-pound behemoth on my shoulders. "But, if there's a redneck with a machine gun at the door, we're coming up with a plan B."

Wes laughs and spins me around to face him, gripping me by the shoulders so the pack doesn't take me down. The way he's looking at me right now, the way his strong hands feel on my body, the way his hopeful smile causes an entire swarm of butterflies to take flight in my belly, I'd probably face down five tattooed rednecks with machine guns if that was what it took to keep him happy. But I don't tell him that.

A girl has to play a *little* hard to get.

CHAPTER 13

Wes

I HAVE TO CUT through the Burger Palace parking lot on my way to the highway. The line of people waiting to get in wraps around the building at least twice, but it's hard to tell through all the fistfights. His royal highness, King Burger, is smiling down at the yelling, kicking, screaming, chest-shoving, hair-pulling mob from his throne up on the digital Burger Palace sign. I've always hated that motherfucker, even as a kid. I remember the way his glowing face would laugh at me as I dug through his dumpsters.

Rich prick.

I swerve to avoid hitting a naked toddler in the middle of the parking lot.

As I slow down to turn onto the highway, I notice that one of the floor-to-ceiling windows on the front of the library across the street has been broken out. A techno beat so loud I can hear it over my engine is pouring out of the place, and inside, colored lights are swirling around like it's a rave. I imagine a bunch of teenage kids inside, guzzling cough syrup and passing out STDs like party favors, but as I pull onto the highway, a topless grandma comes stumbling out, holding what I swear to God looks like a—

"Dildo!" Rain screams, pointing directly at the old lady as we pass by.

I laugh and shake my head. "Guess the Franklin Springs orgy is BYOD."

I don't think I said it loud enough for Rain to hear me through my helmet, but she cackles and smacks me on my good shoulder.

"BYOD!" she squeals. "Oh my God, that thing was, like, a foot long!"

I twist the throttle and take off, causing her arms to snap back around my body and her fingertips to dig into my sides. It's fucking stupid, but I don't like Rain paying attention to somebody else's cock. Even if that cock is made of rubber and belongs to Abraham Lincoln's widow.

It's getting harder and harder to navigate the highway, not just because of the abandoned and wrecked vehicles every ten feet, but because—thanks to the overflowing dumpsters and trash cans all over town—the road is now covered in garbage, too. I really have to slow down and concentrate to avoid hitting something, but that doesn't stop me from glancing up when we pass Rain's house.

It looks exactly the way it did last night, except now there's a baseball-sized hole in the middle of the glass window on the front door.

Crazy bitch. I smirk.

As we drive past, I wonder what the hell went on in there last night. Rain seemed so upset when she came back from getting all those supplies, but while I was sleeping, she turned around and went right back in. Maybe she waited until her dad passed out. Or maybe her mom really did come home. Or maybe she just—

Bam!

A bump under the tires pulls my attention back to the road, and suddenly, it feels like I'm trying to drive through quicksand. The bike is dragging ass, and I have to grip the handlebars harder to keep the damn thing tracking straight.

"Shit!"

I pull off to the side of the road and want to punch myself in the face. This is exactly what I knew would happen. I let myself get distracted for one fucking second, and now, I have a flat tire. I don't even know what I ran over; that's how checked out I was.

I prop the bike up on the kickstand, yank my helmet off, and turn around, prepared to tell Rain to go the fuck home. I want to scream it at her actually. I want to jam my finger into her perfect little face and make her cry off all that fucking makeup. Maybe then she'll stop following me around like a lost puppy, and I'll finally be able to focus again.

But when I stand up, Rain loses her grip on my torso. Her eyes go wide, and her arms flail in huge circles as she falls off the back of the bike, landing on her giant backpack like an upside-down turtle.

"What the fuck, Wes?" she cries, rolling from side to side in a pathetic attempt to get up.

A laugh from the bowels of my tarnished black soul bursts out of me as I watch her struggling on the ground. She cuts me an *eat shit* look that only lasts a second before she starts laughing, too. When she accidentally snorts like a pig, her hoodie-covered hands fly to her mouth in mortification.

"Just take the pack off!" I cry through my laughter, watching her alternate between struggling to get up and succumbing to her own giggle fit.

Rain pulls her arms out of the straps as I reach down and lift her shuddering body off the ground. The moment she's upright, she falls into my chest, snorting and hiccupping and burying her beet-red face in my freshly washed shirt.

And, just like in the nightmare, her touch is all it takes for me to lose complete control—of the situation, of my willpower, of my own body. Instead of giving her a swat on the ass and sending her home like I know I should, I watch like a prisoner in my own mind as my arms wrap around her tiny shoulders and pull her in closer.

No! What the fuck are you doing, pussy? Cut her loose!

I scream at myself, call myself every name in the book, but the voice in my head is drowned out by the euphoric rush I get from holding this girl. She coils my shirt in both fists. Burrows her face into my neck. Her breath comes in short, hot bursts as she giggles against my skin. Her nose is cold. And all I can do is watch in humiliation as the meat puppet I live inside of tips its face down and smells her fucking hair.

Oh my God, you're pathetic.

Sugar cookies. She laughs like a farm animal. She looks like a discarded porcelain doll that raided a teenage boy's closet. And she smells like fucking sugar cookies.

Let her go, dipshit! Supplies! Shelter! Self-defense! That's *what you need!*

But the warning falls on deaf ears because now my stupid fucking cock has gone rogue, too. Why not? Nothing else is listening to me. It springs to life and rams itself into my zipper, seeking Rain's attention as well. I take a small step back, just enough to keep from shoving my hard-on into her belly like a full-fledged creep, but she responds to my step back with one of her own.

And that's it.

The moment is over.

The laughter is gone.

We drop our arms, and we begin walking.

I carry the backpack and push my bike—the front tire almost completely flat—as Rain falls in step beside me. I'm still hard, and I probably will be forever, thanks to the way she's blushing and twirling her hair in her fingers. I decide to concentrate on watching the road for debris—what I should have been doing in the first place.

"So ... how much farther until we get to the hardware store?" I ask, staring at the pavement in front of me.

"Uh ..." Rain looks off in the distance like she can see it.

This part of the highway is nothing but old farmhouses, like hers, with a few untended fields and a shit-ton of trees in between them. No one is growing anything. No one even has horses on their land. Just a bunch of junk cars and a few rusty old sheds.

"Maybe, like, fifteen, twenty minutes? It's on the other side of this hill, down past the skating rink."

I chuckle and shake my head.

"What?"

"You just sounded so country."

Rain scoffs. "If you think *I* sound country, then you haven't heard—"

"No, it's not your accent," I cut her off. "It's just the way everybody down here tells you the distance in minutes instead of miles and uses landmarks instead of street names."

"Oh my God." Rain's mouth falls open. "We *do* do that!"

I smile even though my bullet wound is starting to scream from pushing my bike up this never-ending hill.

She tilts her head to one side, watching me. "You said *everybody down here.* Where were you before you came back? Somewhere up north?"

"You could say that." I smirk, giving her a half-second of eye contact before resuming my death glare at the littered pavement. "I lived in South Carolina for a while, but before that, I was in Rome."

"Oh, I think I've been to Rome. That's close to Alabama, right?"

I snort. "Not Rome, Georgia. Rome, Italy."

"No way!"

Rain reaches over and smacks me on the arm, narrowly missing my bullet wound. I wince and suck in a breath, but she doesn't even notice.

"Oh my God, that's amazing, Wes! What were you doing in Italy?"

"Being a colossal piece of Eurotrash mostly."

Rain leans forward, devouring my words one by one like kernels of popcorn. So, I just keep spewing them.

"After I left Franklin Springs, I never stayed anywhere longer than a year—a few months usually—and then I'd get bounced to the next piece-of-shit house in the next piece-of-shit town. As soon as I aged out of the system, I knew I wanted to get as far away from here as fucking possible. I was sick of small towns. Sick of school. Sick of having no fucking control over where I went or how long I stayed. So, on my eighteenth birthday, I checked all the airline sales, found a last-minute deal to Rome, and the next morning, I woke up in Europe."

"The system?" Rain's dark eyebrows bunch together. "Like foster care?"

"Uh, yeah. Anyway"—I kick myself for letting that slip. It's not that I'm embarrassed about it. I just don't particularly want to talk about the worst nine years of my life right now. *Or ever*—"Rome is fucking incredible. It's ancient and modern, busy and lazy, beautiful and tragic, all at the same time. I had no idea what I was gonna do once I got there, but as soon as I stepped off the plane, I knew I was gonna be all right."

"How?" Rain is so engrossed in my story that she steps on a muffler lying in the street and almost busts her ass.

I try not to laugh. "Almost everybody was speaking English. There were signs in English, menus in English, the street musicians were even playing pop songs in English. So … I cashed in my dollars for euros, bought a spare guitar off one of the street performers, and spent the next few years strumming classic rock songs in front of the Pantheon for tips."

I glance over, and Rain is staring at me like *I'm* the fucking Pantheon. Eyes huge, lips parted. I have to reach out and pull her toward the bike so that she doesn't hit her head on the tire of the flipped Honda minivan we're walking next to.

"Did you have to sleep on the street?" she asks, unblinking.

"Nah, I always found somebody to crash with."

That makes her blink. "Somebody, huh? You mean, some *girl*." When I don't correct her, she rolls her eyes so hard, I half-expect them to fall out of their sockets. "Did you point guns at their heads and make them pay for your groceries, too?"

I raise an eyebrow at her and smirk. "Only the ones who talked back."

Rain scrunches up her nose like she wants to stick her tongue out at me. "So, why'd you leave if you had it so good with your classic rock and your Italian women?" she sasses.

My smile fades. "It was after the nightmares started. Hey, watch out."

I point to a shard of glass sticking up at a weird angle in Rain's path. She glances at it just long enough to avoid it and then returns her rapt attention to me.

"Tourism totally dried up. I couldn't make shit playing on the street anymore, and I couldn't get a real job without a visa. I didn't really have a choice, as usual. My roommate was an American whose parents offered to pay for our plane tickets back to the States, so ... that's how I ended up in South Carolina."

"Did you love her?"

Rain's question catches me completely by surprise.

"Who?"

"Your 'roommate.'" Her big eyes narrow to slits as she makes sarcastic finger quotes around the word *roommate*.

I hate how much I like it.

"No," I say honestly. "Did you love *him*?"

"Who?"

I drop my eyes to the yellow letters emblazoned across her perky tits. "The guy you stole that hoodie from."

Rain's eyes drop to her sweatshirt, and she stops dead in her tracks.

I guess that's a yes.

Crossing her arms over the band logo, Rain lifts her head and stares at something off in the distance behind me. It reminds me of the way she looked when she was watching that family at the park yesterday.

Right before she flipped the fuck out.

Shit.

"Hey … look. I'm sorry. I didn't mean to …"

"That's his house."

Huh?

I follow the direction of her gaze until I'm turned around, staring at a yellow farmhouse with white trim, set back about a hundred feet from the road. It's nicer than her parents' place, bigger, too, but the yard is just as overgrown.

"The boy next door, huh?" I try to keep the malice out of my voice, but knowing that the piece of shit who upset Rain is somewhere inside that house makes me see red.

When Rain doesn't answer, I turn around and find her standing with her back to me. I stomp my kickstand down, prepared to chase her ass if she decides to bolt again, but the rattle of pills against plastic tells me that Rain isn't going anywhere.

She's found a different form of escape.

Rain pops a painkiller into her mouth and shoves the bottle back inside her bra. The whole time, I can practically hear the blood rushing to my extremities.

Whoever this kid is, he's gonna die.

"Rain, I need you to give me one good reason why I shouldn't storm up those steps, drag this punk out by the throat, and force him to eat his own fingers after I cut them off with my pocketknife."

Rain lets out a sad laugh and turns to face me again. "Because he's gone."

I blow out a breath. *Thank fuck.*

"He left with his family a few weeks ago. They wanted to spend *April 23* in Tennessee, where his parents are from," Rain scoffs and rolls her eyes.

April 23. That's what people call it when they don't want to say *the apocalypse.* Like it's a fucking holiday or something.

Rain looks back at me with a mixture of heartbreak and hate in her narrowed eyes, and fuck, do I know that feeling. The hate makes the heartbreak easier to take. Or, at least, it did for me.

Now, I don't feel it at all.

Reaching across my bike, I wrap an arm around her shoulders and pull her toward me. Rain leans across the pleather seat to hug me back, and both my heart and cock swell in response. All I want to do is kiss the shit out of her until she forgets that this idiot farm boy ever existed, but I don't. Not because she's too vulnerable. But because I don't trust myself to stop.

"Hey. Look at me," I say, trying my hardest not to smell her fucking hair again.

Two big blue irises peek up at me from under two black-smudged eyelids, and the need I see in them makes my soul ache.

"Take it from somebody who's a professional at getting left …" I force a grin. "All you gotta do is say *fuck 'em* and move on."

"I don't know how." Rain's eyes are pleading, begging for something to take the pain away.

I recognize the look, but I don't even remember what it feels like anymore.

Because I'm the one who does the leaving now.

Pain doesn't even know my forwarding address.

"It's easy." I smirk. "First, you say, *fuck*. Then, you say, *'em*."

Rain smiles, and my eyes drop to her lips. They're dry and swollen from almost crying, and when they whisper the words, "Fuck 'em," I swear, I almost come in my pants.

"Good girl," I whisper back, unable to look away from her mouth. "Now, let's go light his house on fire."

"Wes!" Rain squeals, smacking me on the chest with a tiny smile. "We're not lighting his house on fire."

She turns and starts walking toward the hardware store again, and I let her lead the way. Not because I don't want to torch that little shit's house. I do.

But because there is a dead woman staring at me from behind the wheel of that overturned minivan.

CHAPTER 14

Rain

BY THE TIME WE get to Buck's Hardware, I feel amazing. The sun is shining, my pills have kicked in, Wes is being nice to me again, and I cannot *wait* to climb that sign and paint a much-needed F over that B.

God, I can't believe I told him about Carter.
What did you expect? You took him right past the guy's house.
I'm such an idiot.
Note to self: take the trail from now on.

I nod to myself as I follow Wes across the parking lot. He's all serious again, slowing down and reaching for his gun as we approach the busted front door. God, it must be exhausting, trying to survive the apocalypse.

I'm just trying to stay high enough to keep from crying all the time, and that's hard enough.

Wes props his bike on the kickstand next to the front door and shoots a warning glance at me over his shoulder. The way he looks reminds me of the way he described Rome. Soft and hard. Old and young. Pale green eyes shadowed by thick, dark brows. Soft brown hair grazing a hard, stubbled jaw. A floral Hawaiian shirt covering jagged black tattoos. I'm attracted to the boy in him and scared of the man in him, and I'm pretty sure I'd take a bullet for both of them even though I don't even know their last name.

But, honestly, I'd probably take a bullet for anybody right about now. This *waiting around to die* thing is killing me.

The glass in the front door has been smashed out, and Wes doesn't seem too happy about it. He pauses against the wall next to the door with his gun drawn and jerks his head, indicating that I'm supposed to join him *next to* the entrance instead of standing right in front of it like a dumbass.

Oh, right.

I hop over to the wall beside Wes, and that's when I hear faint, deep voices inside the building.

Wes turns toward me so that our faces are inches apart, and I hold my breath. I know he's not going to kiss me—that wouldn't even make sense—but my body doesn't seem to know that. It tenses all over and buzzes and hums as Wes's lips graze the edge of my ear.

"I'm gonna give you the backpack so that I can move around more easily in there. You stay out here and watch the bike."

I shake my head violently. "No. I'm coming too."

"No, you're not," Wes hisses between his clenched teeth.

He drops his eyes, and I feel his hand wrap around mine. I look down with my heart in my throat as Wes wraps my fingers around the handle of his gun.

"I won't be able to focus with you in there, and trust me, those guys won't be able to either." Wes's eyes slide up my body to my face, and they take what little power I have along with them. "Stay out here. Please."

I swallow and nod, feeling the weight of his trust fall on my shoulders along with the backpack. Then, he turns and opens the door.

I don't know how he does it, but the glass beneath his feet doesn't even crunch as he tiptoes in and silently closes the door behind him. I watch through the broken glass as he disappears from view.

This is bad.

My painkillers are in full effect, and I can't tell if he's been gone five seconds or five minutes. One of my arms feels heavier than the other.

That's weird. I bend my right elbow and notice a small black handgun in my fist. I blink at it. *How did that get there?*

Thunder booms in the distance even though the sun is shining. Nothing makes sense anymore. I should be in college right now. I should be working part-time at some shitty diner and getting an apartment with Carter and adopting a cat and naming it Blurryface. But, instead, I'm standing outside of Buck's Hardware, holding a gun and guarding a stranger's dirt bike while he sneaks inside to steal a metal detector so that we can find a hidden bomb shelter to live in because the four horsemen of the apocalypse are coming in two days, according to an unexplained dream we've all been having.

I hear the thunder again, only this time, it's coming from inside the building.

Crash!

My heart lurches into my throat as the sounds of struggle—muffled grunts, skin hitting skin, skin hitting the floor, merchandise hitting the floor—come pouring out through the hole in the door. I don't think; I just react. I yank on the handle with my free hand and charge inside, my giant backpack jostling with every step. This place hasn't been ransacked like Huckabee Foods, but on the left side of the store an endcap shelf of fertilizer has been knocked over, and there are plastic containers and little round granules everywhere.

I run in that direction. I don't see anyone yet, but I hear Wes's voice coming from the back of the store.

"Rain, get the fuck out!"

"Rain?" another masculine voice says.

I recognize it immediately.

"Quint?" I almost slip in the spilled fertilizer as I turn the corner and find Quinton Jones, my buddy since kindergarten, standing at the end of the aisle with his daddy's hunting rifle trained on Wes.

Wes has his back to me and appears to be holding Lamar Jones, Quint's little brother, like a human shield. I can't tell from here, but the way his arm is poised, my guess is that he has a certain pocketknife pressed to Lamar's throat as well.

"Quint!" I squeal. "I didn't know you guys were still in town!"

My classmate keeps his gun trained on Wes, but his dark features pull up into a big grin when he sees me. "Rainbow Williams! Got-damn! Where you been, fam?"

I make a beeline for my buddy, but the second I get within arm's reach of Wes, he grabs me, shoving Lamar toward his brother and using me as a human shield instead. I don't even realize he's taken the gun back until I see it stretched out in front of us, aimed at Quint.

Wes's breath is warm against my cheek when he says, "You can tell him hi from here."

I laugh in surprise and wave at the kid I used to play Power Rangers with on the playground. "Hi, Quint." I giggle. "This is my new friend, Wes. Wes, this is Quint and Lamar. Quint was in my grade at school." I turn my head toward Wes and whisper loud enough for everyone to hear, "He's a lifer."

Quint rolls his black-brown eyes at me and elbows his brother. "Here we go with this shit again."

Lamar works his jaw back and forth, which I can now see looks a little swollen, and glares at Wes. He's grown his hair out since the last time I saw it. The top is in short dreadlocks now. I like it.

Wes holsters his gun but keeps his left arm wrapped tightly around my shoulders. I like that, too.

"So, you don't believe in the nightmares?" he asks Quint. His tone is lighter, friendlier.

I know what he's doing. And it seems to be working.

Quint lowers the rifle, stabbing it into the ground like a cane, and launches into one of his numerous conspiracy theories. "All you have to do is look at who's dyin' and who's gettin' rich to know that there's some fucked up shit goin' on. If you ask me, I think this whole thing, the nightmares and all of it, was planned by the government to get all the poor folks and the brown folks to kill each other off. Let the trash take itself out, you know?"

"Yeah, and the Burger Palace CEO is in on it," Lamar chimes in.

His voice sounds deeper than I remember. I don't know if it's because of puberty or because he's trying to sound tough in front of Wes. Either way, it's kinda funny.

Wes snorts in agreement. "That motherfucker is making a killing."

I laugh. "For real! They tried to charge me, like, eighty-seven dollars to *Apocasize* my meal yesterday!"

"See?" Lamar raises his hand in my direction. "That's what I'm talkin' about!"

Quint pushes Lamar's arm back down. "So, what brings y'all to Buck's Hardware on this fine day?" he asks, eyeing us a little more suspiciously.

Wes tilts his head in the direction of the front door. "My bike got a flat."

"And we need a metal detector," I blurt out, earning me a glare and a shoulder squeeze from Wes.

Oops.

"A metal detector?" Quint repeats, raising an eyebrow.

"Y'all lookin' for buried treasure?" Lamar chuckles and cups his swelling jaw with a wince.

"Yeah. I'm pretty sure my dad's got all kinds of stuff buried in the backyard. Y'all know him."

Quint and Lamar smirk and give each other a knowing look. Everybody in this town thinks Phil Williams is a crazy, old, drunken hermit who doesn't leave the house. They're not exactly wrong.

"What about you?" I ask, trying to steer the conversation away from the subject of my dad as quickly as possible.

"Just came in to grab some motor oil." Quint gives Lamar the same look that Wes just gave me, but Lamar ignores him. "We're gettin' outta here."

"Really? How?" I ask. "The roads are so bad; we couldn't even get from Burger Palace to here without a flat."

Lamar grins. "Oh, we ain't worried 'bout flats."

Quint glares at his brother, who isn't getting the hint, and then turns his attention toward me. "Well, we best be goin'." His dark eyes flick from me to Wes and back again. "You good?"

There's something in his tone that tells me he wouldn't hesitate to put a bullet in this white boy if I asked him to. I love him for that.

I glance over my shoulder at Wes and smile. "Yeah, I'm good."

Wes doesn't let me go until the door shuts behind Quint and Lamar. Then, he spins me around and grips my shoulders so hard I feel like he's going to crush them in his bare hands. I wince and brace myself for the lecture that I know is coming about *blah, blah, blah, you never listen, blah, blah, blah, I told you whatever*, but instead, I hear Wes suck a deep breath in through his nose and exhale it just as hard. I open one eye and peek at him. His jaw is clenched, his eyes are narrowed, but he's not yelling. Not yet anyway.

I lift my other eyelid and give him a tiny cringe of a smile. "Don't be mad. I know you said—"

But before I can finish my apology, Wes pulls my body flush against his and smashes his lips even harder against mine. My body goes rigid for a second, completely caught off guard, but when he grabs the back of my head and slides his warm tongue into my gasping mouth, an atom bomb of desperation goes off inside of me. I press up onto my tiptoes and kiss him back, sparklers and bottle rockets going off behind my eyes. Wes tears the backpack off my shoulders and tosses it to the ground before slamming me up against the shelves of weed killer behind me. I can feel him everywhere. His hands are clutching the back of my neck, cupping my face, gripping my waist, grabbing my ass. His chest is pressed against my chest. His thigh is shoved between my legs, and when he rocks his hips forward, I feel another part of him—full and hard— against the side of my belly.

"Wes." My plea is barely audible as it disappears into his relentless mouth.

Wes responds by gripping my hips and grinding against me harder. I feel my core coil and tighten as the entire world, both inside my mind and outside this store, disappears.

"You never ... fucking ... listen," he growls between kisses.

"I know," I pant, hooking my knee over his hip and shifting so that his hardness is now between my legs. "I'm sorry."

Wes's pace becomes even more punishing. I cling to his shoulders and suck on his swirling tongue and hold my breath as tiny earthquakes begin to rock my body. My legs tremble as the pressure builds.

"Wes ..."

I tilt my hips forward, taking the full brunt of his force. Feeling him there—*right there*—separated by only a few layers of fabric and knowing he's just as desperate for me as I am for him, does me in. I whimper against his lips and pulsate around nothing as the earth shifts beneath me, and I'm suddenly falling.

But I don't hit the ground.

The shelf does.

Along with about two hundred plastic jugs of weed killer.

I open my eyes at the sound of the crash to find Wes smirking down at me, lips swollen and eyes hooded. He has a death grip on one of my arms, which he releases slowly as I turn and look behind us at the damage.

My cheeks burn white-hot when I realize what just happened. How pathetic I am. Wes is a sex god, and I just came in my panties and knocked over a shelf of weed killer from a kiss. I can't even face him.

Thunder booms outside—for real this time—and I feel his stubble graze my cheek.

"As much as I'd love to pick up where we left off, I think it's about to rain. We'd better go." He smacks me on the ass and walks off, giving me and my bright red face a much-needed moment to compose ourselves.

So ... that happened, I think, staring down at the damage we did.

I wait for my next thought to come—for me to overanalyze every aspect of that interaction; for me to admire the way the shelves were spaced just far enough apart so that, if one fell, it wouldn't cause a domino reaction; for me to freak out and find a way to make the whole awkward situation worse—but there's nothing inside my head except for a warm, soft, fuzzy kind of glow. I wait and wait, blinking at our mess, smiling to myself, but still nothing comes.

I don't know how long I stand there, admiring the emptiness in my mind, but it's the closest thing to relief I've felt in weeks.

Wes managed to do what all the alcohol and painkillers in the world haven't. With nothing more than his body and his attention, he made it all just go away. All the memories. All the loss. All the worthlessness and loneliness and hopelessness and fear. For a few minutes, I was free of it all.

God, I hope he does it again.

As I wander the aisles of Buck's Hardware, I let my mind actually contemplate the possibility of survival. Maybe living a little longer wouldn't be so bad ... if I were with Wes. Maybe we could make each other happy in our bomb shelter built for two. Maybe, once we find it, we can do what we just did again but without clothes on.

Blurry, grainy images of Carter's boyish face begin to tiptoe around the edges of my chemically induced bliss. He's only been gone about a month, but I can hardly remember what he looked like anymore. What his voice sounded like. What it felt like when we'd sneak out and make love on a blanket under the stars, hidden by the waist-high grass in Old Man Crocker's untended field.

It hadn't felt like whatever Wes just did; I know that much. Or had it? I can't remember.

I walk two or three laps around the store in a daze before I spot Wes kneeling next to his dirt bike just outside the front door. He tucks his hair behind his ear as he fiddles with the tire, and I can't help but admire his gorgeous profile. It's crazy to think that somebody that beautiful came out of Franklin Springs. I'm glad he got out when he did. He doesn't belong here. The people here are ... simple. Or, at least, they *were* before the nightmares began. Now, most of them have left town, killed themselves, or gotten themselves killed.

Not that I'm one to judge. I was thinking about doing one of those three things myself—until Wes showed up.

I take another lap, actually paying attention to the merchandise this time, and discover that Buck's Hardware does not carry metal detectors. My hope deflates like the tire on Wes's bike. How am I supposed to tell him that we came all the way out here and got a flat for nothing? I can't. I won't. I just need to think. I close my eyes and try to concentrate, but nothing comes. It's ironic. This whole time, all I've wanted to do was erase everything in my brain, and now that Wes and the painkillers have finally done it, I need the damn thing back.

I wander the store some more, and just when I'm about to admit defeat, I notice a few giant magnets, grouped together on a shelf near the door. They look like round metal weights with a hole in the middle, and the sign below them says they can lift up to ninety-five pounds.

"Thank you, Jesus," I whisper, raising my palms to the drop-tile ceiling.

I find some yellow nylon rope on a different aisle and use a pair of gardening shears to cut off two six-foot-long lengths of it. I thread one through the hole in each magnet and tie it off, figuring that Wes and I can just drag the magnets behind us as we walk through the woods. If they can lift almost a hundred pounds, surely we'll feel a tug if we pass over a big metal door beneath the pine needles. Right? It might work.

It has to work.

I run outside with the backpack and my makeshift magnets-on-a-rope, eager to show Wes my new invention. He looks up at me from where he's reflating his newly patched tire with a hand pump, and all my excitement leaves me in a single breath. Just beyond the store's covered entrance, the sky has gone from bright blue to slate gray. Sizzling yellow lightning bolts shoot out of the clouds in the distance, and big, fat raindrops are hitting the asphalt parking lot so hard it looks like it's boiling.

"You were right about the rain," I mumble, staring at what's become of our beautiful spring afternoon.

A clap of thunder booms so loud and so close it rumbles a piece of glass loose from the broken door. I jump at the sound of it shattering on the concrete behind me.

Wes glances at me over his shoulder.

"Can we ... can you drive that thing in the rain?"

He raises his eyebrows like that was the stupidest question ever asked. "It's a *dirt* bike. A little mud ain't gonna hurt it."

I smile, hearing the country in his voice for the first time.

Guess he's from Georgia after all.

"You afraid of a little rain? 'Cause I can take you home if—"

"No!" I blurt out before reclaiming my chill. "No, it's fine. I don't mind."

Wes gives me the side-eye, then returns to pumping the tire. "The sooner we find that shelter, the better. I have a feeling the locals are about to burn this whole shitty town to the ground."

"What makes you think that?"

"Because I drove through at least twenty other shitty little towns just like this one on my way here from Charleston, and they were all burning. *Including* Charleston. That's why I left."

"Oh."

I'm such a fucking idiot. Wes arrived in Franklin Springs without so much as a toothbrush, and I never even wondered why.

Thanks, hydrocodone.

"You had to leave because of the fires?"

"Yep," Wes replies in a clipped tone, squeezing the tire to test its fullness. "I was living on Folly Island and waiting tables at this little tiki bar." He's not looking at me, but at least he's talking. "The owners were good people. They let me play guitar on the weekends so I could earn extra tips."

Wes talked about playing guitar in Rome, too. I don't know why, but I have such a hard time picturing him as a musician. I mean, sure, he looks like he just walked offstage with that grunge rock hair and effortlessly cool outfit—not to mention, his stupefyingly gorgeous face—but all the artists and musicians I know are sweet and sensitive. Wes isn't even in the same zip code as sweet and sensitive.

"After everything started shutting down," he continued, giving the tire a few more pumps of air, "they said they'd keep serving 'til they ran out of food. I didn't have shit else to do, so I volunteered to help 'em out."

I smile to myself, picturing Wes grouchily waiting tables by the beach in jeans, combat boots, and a Hawaiian shirt—his half-assed attempt at beachwear.

"On Friday night, some locals came barging in, screaming about fires. The phone lines were already down, so by the time word got to us, half the island had already burned ... including the house I'd been living in." Wes screws the cap back on the tire nozzle as the wind changes direction and begins spraying us with sideways rain.

I shield my face with my forearm. "Oh my God, Wes. I'm so sorry. Did anybody get hurt?"

He stands and wipes his dirty hands on his jeans. "My roommate got out with minor burns, but I didn't wait around to find out about anyone else. I traded my wallet and everything in it with my buddy down the street in exchange for his dirt bike, stole a gun and holster out of his closet before I left, and got the fuck out of town." Right on cue, the wind blows Wes's lightweight shirt like a beautiful floral curtain, exposing the deadly weapon he keeps tucked away underneath.

"But I met you Saturday morning."

Finally, Wes looks at me—or *squints* at me, thanks to the spitting, sideways rain. "Drove all night. I figured, if the world's gonna burn, I'd better get my ass underground."

"And here you are."

Wes looks around and raises one dark, unimpressed eyebrow. "Yeah. Here I am."

"You know, I'm kinda glad your house burned down." I smile, clutching the weights even tighter.

The corner of his grumpy mouth curls upward as those liquid green eyes drop to my chest. "Whatcha got there?"

I look down. "Oh! I made metal detectors!" I hold up the large gray discs to show him my ingenious invention. I can't quite feel my face, thanks to all the painkillers, but if I could, I'm sure it would be sore as hell from this stupid grin.

A deep laugh rumbles in Wes's chest. I feel it vibrate through my body, causing every hair to stand at attention. The air is charged—and not just from the thunder and lightning.

Tell me I did good.

Tell me you're proud of me.

Tell me you'll keep me forever and ever.

Wes opens his mouth, but none of those things come out. Instead, he takes two steps toward me, reaches out, plucks the magnets from my hands like they weigh nothing, and says, "I'm kind of glad my house burned down, too."

My smile widens into a maniacal grin. I rear back to tackle-hug him when an explosion so loud it sounds like an atom bomb causes us both to duck and cover. The lightning strike rattles what's left of the glass out of the front doors and reverberates through the metal awning above us like a tuning fork. My ears are ringing so badly; I barely register that Wes is shouting at me. I blink at him and try to shake off my daze.

"That was the fucking roof! Come on!"

Wes spins me around and shoves the magnets into our already-overstuffed backpack. Then, he throws on his helmet and straddles the bike. The second my arms wrap around his middle, he stomps on the kick-start and plunges us face-first into the storm. I point toward a gap in the woods across the street where the trail starts. Then—clinging to Wes with my free hand—I struggle to yank the hood of my sweatshirt out from under the backpack and onto my head as we fly through what feels like a never-ending waterfall. The rain is pounding on us so hard I wonder if it's hailing.

Once we get into the woods, the rain doesn't hurt as much, but it's just as heavy, flooding the trail with thick brown mud.

"Wipe my visor!" Wes shouts back to me, unable to let go of the throttle or the clutch.

I use my left hand like a windshield wiper, but the second I stop, Wes shouts at me to keep doing it.

"Just take it off!" I shout back, but Wes shakes his head in response.

Another bolt of lightning explodes about a hundred yards in front of us. I shriek as sparks fly from the pine tree it struck, followed by cracks and snaps as it crashes to earth.

Skidding sideways, Wes suddenly stops and pulls the helmet off his head. "I can't see shit!"

"Me either," I yell, holding on to him with both hands and pressing my forehead against his back. My hoodie is soaked through, but at least it's keeping the rain out of my eyes.

More crashes pop and echo all around us as dead branches fall from great heights.

Wes mutters something I can't quite hear before taking off again. I hold on tight, keeping my head down as he accelerates. The force of the rain intensifies, telling me that we're not in the woods anymore, so I look up.

And immediately want to vomit.

Wes is barreling across an open field toward the last place I want to be right now.

The one place he knows is empty.

A yellow farmhouse with white trim.

CHAPTER 15

Wes

I DRIVE RIGHT UP onto that little shit's patio and use my helmet to break out the glass in his back door. I hope Rain wasn't lying about his family being out of town. The only thing country folk love more than God is their goddamn guns. This could get ugly.

I reach inside and unlock the deadbolt, grateful that it's the old-school kind that doesn't require a key. Turning around, I find Rain standing on the porch with her hood over her head, staring at the house like it's gonna eat her alive. I grab her by the elbow and yank her inside as another bolt of lightning drops into the woods like a bomb.

Once the door's shut—or what's left of it—I push the wet hair out of my face and stomp across the kitchen. I can't fucking believe this shit. There's a concrete fallout shelter less than a mile away, but I'm standing in a wooden tinderbox in the middle of a lightning storm.

I flip the light switch, and two fluorescent bulbs overhead flicker to life with a dull hum.

At least the power hasn't gone out yet.

I don't even bother checking the water. There's enough of it dumping out of the sky right now to keep us alive forever.

The kitchen is just as countrified as I expected—beige wallpaper with roosters all over it, rooster-shaped cookie jars, little rooster salt and pepper shakers.

"Your boyfriend sure loves cocks," I tease, but when I turn around, Rain is right where I left her, standing by the back door, staring at the puddle spreading under her feet. "You okay?"

Her shoulders are hunched, and her face is completely hidden underneath that dripping wet hood. "I ... I don't wanna be here," she mumbles without looking up.

"Well, that makes two of us." I open the cabinet closest to me. Dishes. *Next.* More dishes. *Next.* Mugs with motherfucking roosters on them. "You think your boyfriend left anything to eat?"

If I thought I had a chance of fucking this girl, I'd stop reminding her of the fact that she has a boyfriend who is still possibly alive, but A) I can't remember the little shit's name, so I have to call him "your boyfriend," and B) based on the fact that we're standing in his *goddamn kitchen* right now, I'm pretty sure sex is off the menu.

A ceramic rooster stares directly into my soul just before I slam the fourth cabinet.

Cockblocked. Literally.

I probably could have driven a little farther and taken us to Rain's house instead, but after the way she acted last night, I know for a fact that she doesn't want to be there either.

"I'm gonna go change," she mutters. Her hiking boots squeak against the linoleum floor as she passes through the kitchen and into the living room.

Her mood is example number four thousand eighty-five of why it's always better to do the leaving than to be left.

After searching the cabinets, drawers, and pantry and finding nothing but roach killer and rooster-themed bullshit, I take a chance on the fridge. I realize it's a long shot, and I'm right. The fucker is cleaned out. The only things inside are a few ketchup packets from Burger Palace and half a stick of butter. But the freezer, I think I heard angels singing when I opened that thing. Ice cream, corn dogs, frozen waffles, sausage biscuits, steamer bags of vegetables, and the cherry on top ... a frosty half-full bottle of Grey Goose vodka.

This fucker's mom just became my new hero, rooster collection and all.

I unscrew the cap and help myself as a little rag doll appears in the doorway. Her face looks absolutely dejected as she stands there, wearing a Franklin Springs High basketball jersey and shorts and holding a sopping wet bundle of clothes out in front of her.

"What the fuck are you wearing?" I cough, wiping my mouth with the back of my hand.

"It's all I could find," she snaps, a blush staining her cheeks as she glances down at the uniform hanging off her curves. Her voice is quiet and remorseful, but I don't give a shit.

Rain is mine. I stole her. I'm using her. I made her come less than an hour ago, and I don't appreciate her parading around in front of me with some other asshole's jersey on.

"His fucking name is on your back."

"It's all I could find!" she shouts, surprising me with her sudden anger. "He took everything!"

I have a feeling we're not talking about clothes anymore, so I pull open the freezer door, hoping to change the subject before things get heavy again. "Not *everything*."

Rain's eyes go wide, and her little mouth falls open. "Corn dogs?" she whispers, her gaze shifting from me to the bounty in the freezer and back.

"And ice cream … if you eat your veggies." I pull out a steamer bag of frozen broccoli and pop it into the microwave across from the fridge. My stomach growls louder than the thunder outside at the prospect of eating a hot meal. I don't know if it's closer to lunch or dinnertime, but I'm pretty sure the protein bar I shoved into my face this morning was the only thing I've eaten all day.

"Oh my God, a real dinner." The awe in her voice makes me want to puff up my chest with pride even though all I'm doing is pressing buttons on a microwave.

"I'm, uh … gonna do some laundry. You want me to wash that?" Rain's gaze slides down my body, reminding me that my clothes are dripping wet and splattered with mud.

"Sure." I bite the inside of my cheek, trying not to smirk. If this bitch wants my clothes, she can have them.

Unlacing my boots, I step out of each one and leave them in a muddy heap in the middle of the kitchen. Then, I pull my shirt off, nice and slow, and try not to wince when my sopping wet bandage comes off with it. Rain doesn't notice though. In fact, she's not looking at my face or my shoulder at all. She's staring directly at my abs. My white tank top is glued to my chest like I'm in a wet T-shirt contest, so I flex shamelessly as I take off my holster and set it on the counter, followed by everything in my pockets.

I'm not stupid. I know I look like every girl's wet dream, and I use it to my advantage whenever possible. My looks and my resourcefulness are the only tools I've been given in this life. Everything else I've had to beg for, borrow, or fucking steal. Including the little black-haired tool drooling in front of me.

Unbuttoning my jeans, I hear Rain giggle. Not exactly the reaction I was hoping for. I look up to find her beaming—eye makeup ruined from the rain, hair towel-dried and shaggy. She's a mess and a mindfuck, but when she smiles, it steals the air from my lungs.

"More flowers?" She chuckles, her eyes glued to my crotch.

Glancing back down, I realize that I'm wearing my floral-print boxer shorts, the ones my asshole roommate gave me as a joke for Christmas.

"They came with the uniform." I smirk, pushing my jeans the rest of the way down. That shuts her up.

Rain's eyes go wider as she drinks in the outline of my semi-hard cock, plastered down by the clinging fabric of my wet boxers.

His name might be emblazoned across her back, but her nipples are straining against the fabric because of *me*.

I step out of my jeans and hook my thumbs into the waistband of my boxers. Just as I'm about to slide them down, Rain squeezes her eyes shut and squeals. Dropping the bundle in her hands to the floor, she suddenly grabs the sides of her basketball shorts and yanks them down. The jersey is long enough to cover her ass, but I still get a clean shot of those full, perfect tits when she bends over to step out of the shorts.

"Here!" she chirps, holding the shiny blue fabric out toward me with her eyes still closed. "Put these on!"

I chuckle as I toss my wet clothes onto the pile at her feet. As I stalk toward Rain, wearing nothing but a self-satisfied grin, I'm one hundred percent confident that she's forgotten all about What's-his-face. At least, for now. Hell, the way she's blushing and biting that plump bottom lip as I approach, she might have forgotten her *own* name.

I take the shorts from her hand and step into them, taking my sweet-ass time. Once they're on, I clear my throat, prompting Rain to open her eyes. I'm crowding her space, so close she has to crane her neck back to look up at me. The microwave dings, but neither of us pays it any attention.

"Thanks."

Her eyes drop to my chest. I know without looking what she's staring at. I can see her counting.

"Thirteen?"

It was the first tattoo I ever got. Thirteen jagged tally marks, right above my heart. Usually, when girls ask about it, I just make some shit up. *Thirteen is my lucky number.* Or, *My mom's birthday was August thirteenth.* Or, *It's the number of touchdown passes I threw to win the state championship back in high school.*

But Rain isn't going to fuck me, no matter what I say—at least, not in this house—so I tell her the truth.

"It's the number of foster homes I was in."

She doesn't bat an eye at my admission. She just lets them roam over my flesh. "What about this one?"

She's staring at the rose and dagger on my right shoulder, just above my bullet wound. I laugh. "Have you ever heard that song 'Eurotrash Girl'?"

Rain nods and looks up at me.

"Well, there's a part where he talks about getting a tattoo of a rose and a dagger in Berlin, so one weekend, when some friends and I took the train to Berlin for Oktoberfest, we all got rose and dagger tattoos."

"Uh, I'm pretty sure he talks about getting crabs in Berlin, too." Rain wrinkles her nose and gives me the side-eye. "Or was that Amsterdam?"

"No, I think Amsterdam's where he sold his plasma."

"Right." She grins. "And spent all the money on a guy in drag."

"It happens to the best of us." I shrug, eliciting another giggle from Rain.

"What's the story behind this one?" Her eyes drift down to my elbow.

I roll my arm over, showing the whole thing.

I snort a laugh through my nose. "I had a buddy who wouldn't let his tattoo artist go near his elbow because he heard it was the most painful place to get inked, so while he was getting some work done on his bicep, I got another artist at the shop to do a bull's-eye right on my elbow, just to be a dick."

Rain laughs, the smile finally reaching her eyes. "Did it hurt?"

"Like a bitch."

Water from the clothes on the floor trickles over to my bare feet as Rain's eyes devour the stories etched in my skin. I wanted to use my body to taunt her, punish her, but instead, she's reading it like an open book. When her gaze slides over to the wilted lily tattoo on my ribs, I've never felt more exposed.

"Did that one hurt?" She touches it with a cold fingertip, tracing the stem down my side.

"Yeah." I swallow. "Every fucking day of my life."

Her eyebrows pull together as she searches my skin for signs of injury. Gentle fingers skate over the drooping pink petals—one for every month of her short life.

"Lily was my sister." I don't even know why I'm telling her. Maybe so that she'll stop fucking touching me like that.

Rain lifts her head but not her fingers. Those she splays over my ribs, covering the ink like a bandage.

"I'm sorry." The sincerity in her big blue eyes is so genuine, the hurt in her voice so raw, I get the sense that Rain isn't sympathizing with me. She's commiserating.

The microwave dings a reminder, and I couldn't be more thankful for the interruption.

"Show's over," I call over my shoulder as I walk toward the beeping machine.

A cloud of steam hits me in the face when I open the door. Setting the bag of cooked broccoli on the counter, I spin around to grab the rest of our dinner out of the freezer.

"You wanted a corn dog, right?"

I grab a box of corn dogs and a few individually wrapped sausage, egg, and cheese biscuits. Then, I turn toward Rain. Her mouth is open in a way that makes me want to put something inside of it. Food will do. My tongue would do better. My dick would be a fucking miracle.

"I'll take that as a yes." I smirk.

Rain blinks the emotion off her face and scoops the bundle of clothes off the floor, inadvertently flashing me again in the process. I snicker as I watch her scamper into the laundry room on the far side of the kitchen.

I return my attention to the glowing microwave and try not to think about the tingling sensation left on my skin where

Rain's cold hand just was. A hollow, metallic clang and repetitive swishing sounds from the washing machine signal her return. Rain says nothing as she stands beside me, our stomachs growling in unison as we watch our processed meat products twirl under the halogen lights.

Then, one wall-rattling clap of thunder brings it all to a standstill. With a flash and a rumble, the house goes dark. The dance stops. And those once-blinking numbers on the microwave disappear for good.

"Shit." I open the door and pull out our food. It's still cold to the touch, but it seems thawed at least.

A gust of wind whips through the broken back door, causing Rain to shiver and cross her arms over her chest.

"Does ..." I'm about to say *your boyfriend* but stop myself at the last minute. "Does *this house* have a fireplace?"

Rain nods, staring at her corn dog like it's a beloved family member on life support.

"It's gonna pull through," I tease, squeezing her shoulder. Which earns me a smack on the arm.

Fuck, that hurt. I make a mental note to ask Rain to patch me up again tonight. My bullet wound is starting to throb like a motherfucker.

I grab my lighter, the broccoli, and the bottle of vodka and follow Rain out of the kitchen, focusing on her round ass instead of the name above it. The living room has a vaulted ceiling and has been decorated with plaid furniture and the heads of decapitated animals. Not exactly my taste, but the fireplace is nice. It's big and stone and filled with actual logs. Not those fake-ass gas-burning things.

I place everything on the hearth and grab a *Field & Stream* magazine off the coffee table. Ripping out a few pages, I twist them into a stick and light the end on fire. Rain sits cross-legged on the carpet beside me, careful to keep the jersey tucked between her legs. She's holding the corn dog in one hand and the biscuits in the other.

"Just so you know …" I say, holding the makeshift torch against the smallest piece of wood until it catches. "Mine's bigger."

Rain furrows her thin eyebrows at me and then bursts out laughing when my eyes shift from her face to the breaded wiener in her hand.

Fuck, I love that sound.

"Why are you in such a good mood?" She smiles as I take the food from her and lay it on the hearth to warm up.

"Because I'm about to eat the shit out of these biscuits."

And because nobody's trying to kill me at the moment.

And because I might get to sleep in an actual bed tonight.

And because I got to see your tits … twice.

"This whole time, I thought you were a jerk, and it turns out, you were just hangry?"

"Oh, I'm still a jerk." I grab the bottle of vodka off the hearth and press the ice-cold glass against her outer thigh just to make my point.

"Ahh! Okay, okay! You're still a jerk!" she screams, swatting it away.

I chuckle and twist off the cap, giving her a salute with the neck of the bottle before tipping it back. The vodka goes down smooth, dulling away the hard edges of the day.

I extend the bottle toward Rain but pull it back at the last second. "Just a sip, okay? You're on that Hydro shit, and the last thing I need is for you to puke or die."

Rain smiles as she accepts my offering, and something warm spreads inside my chest that has nothing to do with the fire or the alcohol. As I watch her eyelids flutter shut and her pretty pink lips wrap around the frosty glass bottle, I wish like hell that it were me. Any part of me. Every part of me.

"That's enough," I bark, snatching it out of her hand.

She laughs and coughs against the back of her wrist. "God, I hate vodka."

"What else do you hate?" I ask, surprisingly interested in learning more about my newly acquired resource.

I tear open the bag of broccoli and set it on the carpet in front of us. Rain's hand plunges inside, pulling out a fistful of little green trees.

"I'm fucking starving," she mumbles, popping one into her mouth.

"You didn't answer my question."

She shrugs. "I don't know … everything?" I watch the joy drain from her face as she stares into the fire. "All of this. This town, the nightmares, what they make people do, just waiting around to die. I hate all of it."

"You wanna know what I hate?" I ask, nudging her with my elbow. "Actually, it's more of a who."

"Who?" she croaks, clearing the emotion from her throat.

"Tom Hanks."

"Tom Hanks!" Rain squeals and shoves my leg. "Nobody hates Tom Hanks! He's the nicest guy in America!"

"I call bullshit," I say, leaning forward to rustle the logs with a fire poker. "It's all just an act. I'm not falling for it."

Rain snorts like a pig—*again*—which makes her laugh even harder, and I realize this is the most fun I've had in a long time. I poke one of the biscuits on the hearth and decide that our dinner is warm enough.

Thunder booms off in the distance as I hand the dick-on-a-stick to Rain. She grins and bites the tip off.

"Savage." I cringe.

We both go quiet as we inhale our meals. As the minutes stretch on, I can almost see our thoughts accumulating on the carpet between us, heavy and dark.

The dirty ones are mine.

I wonder how many little pricks from high school stuck their dick in that perfect mouth. How many of them were invited and how many just took advantage of a pretty little throwaway. I wonder what she would be doing right now if I hadn't pulled her out of Burger Palace. What she would be doing if the nightmares had never started. I wonder if she's going to go home again in the middle of the night or if she'll spend the whole thing here with me.

Rain's cheeks, full of food, flush pink when she catches me staring. "What?" Her voice is defensive as she brushes invisible crumbs away from her mouth.

"I'm just trying to figure you out."

"Good luck. I've been tryin' for years." Rain slides the last bite of corn dog off the stick with her fingers and pops it into her mouth.

"What were you like in high school?"

"I dunno." She shrugs. "Blonde."

"Blonde?" I snort.

"That was the only thing I was ever good at. Being blonde. Being pretty. Being a perfect little trophy. I wasn't real outgoing, so most people just thought I was a stuck-up bitch, but I got good grades. I made my mama proud. I dated the basketball star and went to church every Sunday. You know, small-town shit."

As she talks, I begin to see glimmers of that girl in the one I'm looking at. The mascara smudged under her eyes. The half-inch of blonde roots I never noticed before. The killer fucking curves she was hiding under all that baggy clothing. Rainbow the bombshell became Rain the badass.

But both of them are just disguises.

I snap my fingers as it hits me. "You're a chameleon."

Rain gives me an offended glare. "What, like I'm fake?"

"No. You're *adaptive*. You change how you look to suit your environment, to survive, like a chameleon."

Rain rolls her eyes at me. "And what are *you*?"

"Me?" I point to myself with the bottle of vodka in my hand. "I'm good at figuring people out." I give her a wink and take another swig. Wincing from the burn, I twist the cap back on. "Guess it's a by-product of changing homes every six to twelve months."

I set the bottle down on the carpet next to me, but when I glance back over at Rain, she's not looking at me anymore. She's staring at the corn-dog stick in her hands.

"Wes?" she asks, twirling the wood between her fingers.

"Yeah …"

Rain tosses the stick into the fire. It flickers blue as it catches, probably from all the fucking chemicals and preservatives.

"What happened to your sister?"

Fuck.

I swallow and decide to just rip the Band-Aid off.

"She starved to death."

There. I said it. Let's move on.

Rain's eyes shoot open as she turns to face me. "What?" She shakes her head, confusion rippling her forehead. "How?"

"Neglect." I shrug. "She was only eight months old. My mom was an addict and could hardly take care of herself, and our dads were both out of the picture. I managed to get myself to school and scavenge for food in the dumpster behind Burger Palace, but I never once thought about feeding my sister. She was just a baby, you know? I didn't even think she ate food."

"Oh my God, Wes."

Rain's mouth falls open like she's going to say more, but I cut her off, "She used to cry all the time. *All* the fucking time. I would play in the woods or at my friends' houses every chance I got so that I wouldn't have to hear it. Then, one day, the crying just … stopped."

I remember the relief I felt, followed by the horror of finding her lifeless body, faceup in her crib.

"The cops came when I called 911, and that was the last time I saw my mom. My case worker said I could go see her in jail, but …"

I shake my head and glance at Rain, waiting for the typical condolences to come pouring out of her parted lips. *I'm so sorry. That's just awful. Blah, fucking blah.* But she's not even looking at me. She's staring into the fire again, a million miles away.

"My mom got pregnant when I was about eight or nine, too."

My stomach drops. Rain never mentioned having a younger sibling, so I'm pretty sure this story doesn't have a happy ending.

"I was so excited. I loved playing with baby dolls, and I was about to have a real one that I could play with every day."

"Did she have a miscarriage?" I ask, hoping the answer is yes.

Rain shakes her head. "My daddy gets real mean when he's been drinking. He never puts his hands on me, but sometimes, when he gets like that, my mama—"

Rain suddenly goes so still. It's as if somebody turned her off. She stops talking. She stops breathing. She even stops blinking. She just stares into that damn fire as all the color drains from her face.

"Rain ..."

She clamps her hands over her mouth and nose, and I know any minute the rocking and hair-pulling are going to begin.

Oh shit.

"Hey." I put a hand on her bare shoulder, but she recoils from my touch. "Rain, tell me what's going on."

She shakes her head, a little too hard. "Nothing," she lies, forcing herself to meet my stare. "I'm just ... I'm really sorry about your sister." The sadness in her voice is sincere, but when she yawns, it's fake as hell. "I'm so tired. I think I'm gonna go to bed, okay?" Rain doesn't even wait for my response before she's practically running out of the room.

What.

The fuck?

I hear a door slam down the hall but no crying. At least, not yet. I'm sure she's too busy digging a little white pill out of a little orange bottle.

Whatever. I am not going after her crazy ass. I'm gonna sit right here, enjoy this fire, drink this entire bottle of vodka, and pass the fuck out.

I take a nice long pull from the ice-cold bottle and hear what sounds like music coming from down the hall.

So what? Maybe she falls asleep listening to music.

Then, I recognize the song—"Stressed Out" by Twenty One Pilots.

Twenty One fucking Pilots.

She's in *his* room, listening to *his* music, wearing *his* clothes, like she still belongs to *him*. But she doesn't, and it's high fucking time that she got that through her head.

Fueled by three or four or six shots of vodka and Rain's erratic behavior, which is obviously contagious, I stand up and stomp down the dark hallway she disappeared into, mad that my bare feet don't make any sound on the worn-out carpet. I want her to hear me coming. I want my footsteps to rattle off the walls.

This bullshit ends now.

My eyes take a second to adjust to the dark. I see three doors in the hallway before it turns left, but only one is shut. I walk right over to it and give it a hard shove. The music gets louder as it swings open, and there, sitting cross-legged in the center of a bare mattress, is Rain, rocking and staring at a glowing MP3 player in her hands.

"Get up," I shout.

Rain jumps. Her head swivels toward me, but she doesn't move.

"I said, get the fuck up!" My voice booms in What's-his-face's tiny bedroom, but I don't even try to rein it in. I don't even think I can right now.

I'm furious that I see a nine-year-old version of myself in her lost eyes, and I want to slap it out of her. I'm furious that something is hurting her, and she won't let me murder it. But mostly I'm furious that I didn't find her soon enough to stop whatever it is from happening in the first place.

Rain hops up, standing next to the bed with the glowing device in her hands, and stares at me. She's not crying. She's not running. And, for the first time since I laid eyes on her, she's awaiting her next command like a good little soldier.

"I need you to get something through that pretty little head of yours right now." I take two steps into the room and point my finger directly at her face. "Everybody ... fucking ... leaves. I don't know what's going on with your family, and honestly, it doesn't matter. Because people are temporary.

Everyone you love, everyone who's hurting you—they will all fucking leave, one way or another. They might die, they might get locked up, or they might just throw you away once they find out how fucked up you are, but they ... will ... leave ... you." I drop my hand and take a breath through my nose, trying to calm myself down.

Shaking my head, I close the distance between us with a final step and continue in a slightly less homicidal tone. "*Our* job ... is to say *fuck 'em* and survive anyway. That's it, Rain. That's our only job. That took me twenty-two years to figure out, and I wish you had twenty-two years to figure it out, too, but you don't. You have two fucking days. So, I need you to man the fuck up because I can't do *my* job without *you*." Emotion—one I don't remember feeling since I was a kid— strangles me, cutting off my voice before the last syllable of my confession.

Rain shakes her head as a new song begins to play. "That's not true." Her voice is quiet but strong. "Because I'm not gonna leave *you*."

The singer begs her to save his heavy, dirty soul, but she drops him onto the bed and buries her face in *my* heavy, dirty soul instead.

Her embrace on my bare chest makes me feel like I've been skinned alive. I'm nothing but raw pink meat in her arms. My scales, my fur, my leathery hide ... it's all been ripped away. Rain's touch penetrates through every layer of defense I thought I had, reaching places that have never seen the light of day. I hate this feeling. Every muscle in my body tenses in response to the pain, but I hold her to me anyway.

Wrapping my arms around her warm, curvy body, I slide a hand up her back and thread my fingers into her short, damp hair. "Oh, I *know* you're gonna leave me," I growl, pulling her head back so that she's looking up at me in the dark. "So, until then, I'm gonna use ... you ... up."

Rain presses up onto her toes at the same moment that I dive for her parted lips, and our mouths collide like the train wreck that we are. I tilt my head sideways and plunge my tongue into her mouth, unable to get my fill. I'm gripping her hair too tight, but I'm powerless to release her. Instead, I slip my free hand under that sad excuse for clothing and grip her full, round ass. My heart jackhammers in my chest as I swallow her responsive moan.

Her hands slide up my back and around to my front, skirting over my pecs and locking behind my neck. I feel her nipples against me, hard as pebbles beneath that unworthy dipshit's jersey, so I pull it off over her head and toss it to the floor. I can barely see her in the darkness, but I don't need to. My hands read the curves of her body as they skim every square inch of her goose bump—covered flesh. She shivers as I knead her perfect tits, and when I break our kiss to pull one perky, needy nipple into my mouth, her hand reaches for me.

She grips me through the silky fabric of the athletic shorts, which were already tented and struggling to contain what she's done to me. My cock is at full attention, swollen and throbbing in her hand, as she gently holds my head to her breast. Her touch is so tender; it causes another surge of emotion to tighten around my throat. It hurts, the way she touches me. It's fucking killing me.

And I'm going to let it.

Rain slides her hand up and down over my shaft through the slippery material as I suck and tongue and worship her other nipple. My every breath on her flesh elicits a reaction, and when I kiss my way back up to her mouth, when I slide both hands over her full ass and tease her slick folds from behind, that reaction is a purr so sweet it vibrates every nerve in my body like a guitar string.

Rain dips her fingers into the waistband of my shorts and guides them down, carefully releasing me. Then, her lips take the same amount of care as they travel from my mouth to my jaw, forging a trail of lingering kisses down my neck and sternum. She takes a step back and bends at the waist as she continues her descent. All I can do is stand here and let her cut me open. That's what her trail of kisses feels like—the slice of a fucking scalpel. She's peeling back my layers, exposing all of my unlovable insides, and she's pretending that she likes what she sees.

But she doesn't. No one ever has, and no one ever will.

The second she sinks to her knees, just before she puts that lying mouth on my cock, I grab her by the hair and pull her head back to face me. "You don't have to do this," I rasp. And, for once, I'm shocked to realize that I mean it.

I want to be inside of her but not like this. This is how the bar flies try to please me. The tourists and college girls and drunken divorcées. They get down on their knees and look up at me like porn stars while they suck me off, practically begging me to fall in love with them.

Daddy issues, all of them.

This bitch has daddy issues, too, and here she is, looking up at me with big, desperate eyes, about to put my cock in her mouth to win my approval ... just like the rest of them.

"You don't want ..." Rain's voice trails off as I drop to my knees, too.

Grabbing the backs of her thighs, I pull her forward until she's straddling my lap. Her tits are flush against my chest, her lips are once again grazing mine, and I've got her plump, round ass in both hands.

"Perfect," I whisper.

Rain smiles against my mouth as she begins to slide her wet pussy along the length of my shaft. I devour that smile. I chew it up and swallow it. And I feel it burn like fire inside of me, illuminating things I thought were gone forever.

Things I hoped would stay that way.

I don't want to press her to have sex. Hell, I don't even know if she's done it before. But, when Rain threads her fingers into my hair and cradles my head in her hands and sinks down onto me with a gasp, I'm suddenly the one feeling inexperienced. This isn't sex. This is so far outside the realm of sex that I don't even know where I am.

All I know is that it hurts. There's pressure everywhere. My chest feels like it's about to explode. My head is pounding.

My eyes burn like I've been pepper-sprayed. And my balls are already tightening in response to Rain's warm welcome.

I wrap my arms around her waist and try to accept everything she's giving me even though it cuts me to the bone. I try to give it back, but I feel clunky and uncoordinated. I don't know how to do what she's doing. I don't even know if there's anything left of me to give.

She's not afraid as she pulls me in fully, grinds against me, and sears me with her napalm kisses. It's like she's done this a hundred times before. And that's when I realize ... she has.

In this very room.

With someone else.

Rain's not making love to *me*. She's making love to *him*.

The pressure I was feeling suddenly disappears. I can breathe again. I'm not in danger. There is no threat. This is simply a transaction—sex in exchange for a little boyfriend role-play.

Well, that's too fucking bad. If Rain wants to fuck somebody, she's gonna have to settle for *me*.

Grabbing her ass with both hands, I rear up onto my knees and chuckle as she squeals and wraps her arms and legs around me. I stand and drop her onto the mattress, crawling over her like a predator as the MP3 player tumbles to the floor. The singer is whining about some girl who left a tear in his heart. I feel bad for the guy. He really shouldn't let himself get that attached.

I form a plank over Rain's body, careful not to touch her as I line myself up with her tight little slit. That's all she's getting from me. *I* do the using in this relationship, and tonight, I'm using her for sex. Boyfriend role-play not included.

The moment I plunge inside of her, Rain wraps her thick thighs around my waist and laces her fingers together behind my neck. "Come here," she whispers, tugging me toward her, and the huskiness in her voice has me dropping to my elbows to kiss her.

Rain's lips are brutally soft. Her touch, too. I thrust into her harder, hoping she'll take the hint and drop the act, but she's determined to make this fantasy happen. I'm just about to flip her over and take her from behind when a single syllable stops me in my tracks.

"Wes ..."

Wes.

Not What's-his-face.

Wes.

"Yeah?" I rasp, that fucking noose tightening around my throat again.

Rain's hands slide to my cheeks. "What's your name? Your whole name?"

I wish I could see her face. I wish I could see the sincere curiosity I hear in her voice shining out of those big blue doll eyes.

"Wesson Patrick Parker." I swallow, but the noose only tightens.

"I thought you might be a Wesson." Rain presses her little feet against my ass and tilts her hips up, drawing me back into her molten heaven.

"What's yours?" I manage to choke out, burying myself in it to the hilt.

"Rainbow Song Williams."

I retreat slowly, missing her with every inch, and thrust back in again. "What does it mean?"

Rain moans softly and wraps her arms around my back. I slide my hands under her shoulders and lie flush on top of her, wondering if she can feel my heart pounding the way I can.

"It's the title of a song by that band, America, from the '70s." Rain nuzzles her face into the side of my neck and plants a kiss there. "It's kinda sad actually. It's about a girl who fell asleep on a rainbow while she was hiding from blowing leaves and broken dreams."

I brace myself on my forearms and look into the reflective pools of her eyes. "It sounds like you." I watch them crinkle at the corners as she smiles, and before she can say another word,

I surprise myself by sitting back on my haunches and pulling her up with me. Rain sinks down onto my dick again, and we're just like we were before—her ass in my hands, her parted lips on mine, and her fingers running through my hair.

Fucking perfect.

Her movements are less tender now. More desperate. Mine feel less awkward, more confident. Rain nips at my tongue with her teeth as she slides up and down on my cock. I slap her ass and grin as she tugs on my hair in response. This isn't what she did in the dark with What's-his-face. This is what she does in the dark with *me*. And, when she moans my name again, I fucking know it.

"Wes," she chants, her voice a breathy plea as her ass slaps against my thighs, and her tight little slit squeezes me even harder. "Wes ..."

The feeling of Rain coming all over my cock with my name on her lips and my head in her hands is unlike anything I've ever experienced before. It shatters me. A tear rips through my heart as I clutch her panting, writhing body—just like that Twenty One Pilots motherfucker said it would—because I want this. I want her. But how can I keep her when everybody fucking leaves?

My hips jerk and my balls tighten as I thrust up into her. I know I should pull out. I always pull out. But, as my dick swells and stiffens inside her pulsating body, I just ... can't. Not this time. Nothing has ever felt more right in my whole fucked up life, so I decide to let myself have it. I'm a selfish bastard, and I want this.

I want Rain.

With a final surge, I coil my arms tighter around her waist and pour everything I fucking have into a girl I just met yesterday. As my cock jerks and spurts hot cum inside her still-trembling body, the pressure in my chest and the noose around my throat fade away, replaced with something warm and fuzzy and completely foreign.

Hope.

CHAPTER 16

April 22
Rain

"THAT ONE LOOKS LIKE a cupcake." I smile, squinting up into the afternoon sky.

Wes and I are lying on a red-and-white-plaid blanket in the middle of Old Man Crocker's overgrown field, watching a parade of clouds float by. He pulls me into his side and kisses the top of my head. I feel it sizzle all the way down to my toes, like a bolt of lightning.

"You're adorable ... because that's clearly the dog shit emoji."

"Oh my God." I giggle. "You're right!"

"I know." Wes shrugs, my head on his shoulder rising and falling along with the movement. "I'm always right."

"What do you think that one is?" I ask, pointing to a human-shaped blob traveling by.

Wes picks a blade of grass and begins twirling it between his fingers. "The one that looks like a guy holding an ax over a teddy bear? Must be Tom Hanks. Fuckin' asshole."

I snort and cover my mouth with my hand.

"You know you sound like a pig when you do that?" Wes teases.

"You know you look like a pig when you eat?" I tease back.

"Guess we're made for each other." Wes lifts my left hand from his chest and slides the blade of grass he was playing with, looped and knotted to look like a ring, onto my fourth finger.

My breath catches as I wiggle my finger in the air, half-expecting it to glint in the sun like a diamond.

I prop myself up on my elbow and smile down at his beautiful face, trying to figure out how somebody who looks like he belongs on a poster in a teenage girl's bedroom could possibly think he was made for me.

Wes props himself up, too, mirroring me, and places a sweet kiss on my grinning mouth. "I can't wait until all of this shit is over, and it's just you and me."

He kisses me again, slower and deeper, sending a jolt of electricity straight between my legs that time. I don't know if I pull him on top of me or if he guides me down, but somehow, I end up on my back again, this time with Wes hovering over me. His hair falls like a curtain over the side of his face, shielding us from the sun.

"I can't wait either," I reply with swollen lips and flushed cheeks. "When it's all over, we should go find a mansion ... up on a hill ... and paint terrible portraits of each other all over the walls."

Wes drops his lips to my neck, just below my ear, and whispers, "What else should we do?"

He kisses me there. Then, a little lower. Then, a little lower. The pillowy softness of his lips combined with the abrasive drag of his stubble causes my toes to curl into the blanket.

"Uh ..." I try to think, but it's difficult with Wes's tongue sliding along my collarbone. "We should find a convertible ... and clear the highway ... and drive it as fast as we can."

Wes makes his way over to my shoulder, sliding the spaghetti strap of my sundress down along his path. "What else?" he murmurs against my heated flesh.

Wes's fingertips graze my skin as he slides the straps of my dress down to my elbows. The thin yellow fabric rolls off my chest, and Wes follows it with a trail of kisses.

"I ..." I don't even know what I'm saying anymore. *My thoughts are scrambled, and my attention is focused completely on the scratchy-soft feel of this beautiful man. I reach up to stroke his silky hair and say the first thing that comes to mind, "I want you to learn how to fly a plane"—I gasp as his curious tongue swirls around my exposed nipple—"and take me somewhere I've never been."*

"Like where?" he asks, continuing his descent, taking my dress and inhibitions with him as he kisses his way down my stomach.

"Somewhere with ... windmills ... and flower gardens ... and-and little thatched-roof cottages." I arch my back involuntarily as I feel the tip of Wes's finger trace the seam of my body over my lace panties.

This is heaven, *I think, feeling the sun's warmth on my skin and Wes's tender touch all the way down to my soul.* That's the only explanation. I died, and this is my reward for letting my mom drag me to church all those years.

"What do you want to do when it's just the two of us?" I ask, glancing down the length of my body.

Wes lifts his mossy-green eyes, narrowed in wicked playfulness and hooded by bold, dark eyebrows. "This," he says before disappearing under my skirt.

"Rainbooooow!" A voice as familiar as the name it's calling floats past us on the wind.

Mom?

I sit up and peek over the top of the tall grass. My mother is standing on our front porch across the street with her hands cupped around her mouth.

"Rainboooow! It's time to come hooooome!"

"Mom!" I struggle to pull my dress up, eager to run to her.

I've missed her so much. But, as I go to stand, the ground begins to rumble. I grab Wes for stability as the knee-high grass shoots up all around us. In seconds, it grows as tall as Wes, caging us in. A ripping sound pulls my attention to our blanket, which is splitting down the middle as more blades of grass burst out of the earth, separating us like the bars of a jail cell.

"No!" I scream, grabbing Wes with both hands. I pull him to my side of the blanket just before the last grassy rod explodes from the ground.

Panting, I glance at his face, expecting to see anger or confusion or that look of focused determination he pulls on when he's trying to hide his feelings from me, but there's just ... nothing.

His features are as expressionless as a wax figure, and his eyes look right through me when he opens his mouth and says, "Time to go home, Rain."

He slowly raises one arm and points to something behind me. I turn and see that a trail has opened up in the side of our grassy, six-foot-high cell.

I exhale in relief and tug on Wes's still-outstretched hand, but his feet are rooted to the ground.

"Come on!" I shout, tugging again. "I'm not leaving you here!"

"Everybody leaves." His voice is monotone as he recites his personal mantra.

I feel like I'm in Oz, and he's the Scarecrow—familiar but confused as he mindlessly points me away from him.

"Rainboooow!" My mom's voice sounds farther away.

We have to go.

"Come on!" I tug on Wes's outstretched hand again, this time yanking hard enough to get his feet moving.

We enter the narrow path, and I have to pull him every single step of the way.

Until it forks.

Shit!

I glance down both trails, noticing that each one appears to end in another fork.

"Give me a boost," I say, walking behind Wes and putting my hands on his shoulders.

He mechanically does as I asked, giving me his hand as a foothold so that I can climb up onto his back. When I peer over the top of the grass, my stomach sinks. Old Man Crocker's field has morphed into a giant, intricate maze. I can still see my mother standing on the porch across the street, but it feels like she's twice as far away now, shielding her eyes from the sun as she looks for me in the field.

"*Mom!*" *I call out, waving my hands above my head.* "*Mom! Over here!*"

Something catches her attention, but it's not me. The earth rumbles again as I turn to follow the line of her gaze. I watch in amazement as a green stem grows up out of the middle of the field, as thick and tall as a telephone pole. Once it's reached its full height, it blooms.

I expect to be dazzled by velvety flower petals or palm leaves the size of water slides, but instead, the stem opens and releases a single black-and-red banner that unfurls all the way to the ground.

My heart plummets along with it, landing in the acid bath of my stomach without so much as a splash.

Three more stems spring from the quaking earth. Three more ominous banners bloom, each depicting a different hooded figure on horseback.

And a date, written at the top in bold.

"*Wes, what day is it?*" *I cry, already knowing the answer but praying for a miracle.*

His body is as rigid as his voice is emotionless when he replies, "*Why, it's April 23, of course.*"

"*Go!*" *I shout, gripping his shoulder and pointing toward my house.* "*Run, Wes! Run!*" *I watch as my mother recoils from the evil banners, walking backward into the house and shaking her head in disbelief.* "*She's gonna leave, Wes!*"

"*Everybody leaves,*" *he recites again, his feet rooted to the spot.*

"*Shut! Up!*" *I scream, hitting him as hard as I can. My blow lands on the side of his head. It feels like I punched a pillow, but when I look down, Wes's head is lying on his shoulder, and straw is sticking out of a huge tear in the side of his neck.*

"*Oh, Wes,*" *I sob, trying to stuff the straw back in.* "*I'm sorry. I'm so sorry.*" *I lift his head back into place and hold it steady with my hands. I realize that his once-shiny brown hair has turned to brittle hay, his skin beige burlap.*

The ground rumbles again.

I'm afraid to look, but my head swivels around anyway. There, at the edge of the field, stand four black horses—eight feet tall at the shoulder, smoke billowing from their flared nostrils—and their faceless, cloaked riders. They don't appear to be pursuing us though, and for a moment, I allow myself to hope that perhaps the field is somehow off-limits to them. I exhale a sigh of relief, but it leaves my throat as a scream when the horseman on the far right lowers his flaming torch to the top of the grass.

"Run!" The word tears out of me as I urge Wes to move, nudging and pushing and kicking his straw-filled body, but he just stands there like the empty scarecrow he is, staring at a wall of grass.

I climb off of him and tug on his lifeless arm. Smoke and flames climb toward the sky behind him as the sound of my mother's motorcycle roars behind me.

"She's leaving! You're gonna burn! Please, Wes! Please come with me!"

Tears blur my vision and burn my cheeks as I stare into the dead button eyes of a soulless man.

"Everybody leaves," he repeats mindlessly. His straw-filled brain unable to listen to reason.

Fire consumes the wall of grass behind him, blacking out the sky with smoke as I tug his arm completely off. Straw flies from the severed sleeve as I toss it into the blaze and wrap myself around his burning, hot waist.

"You're wrong," I sob into his tattered plaid shirt just before it goes up in flames. "I'm not leaving you."

The heat sears the flesh from my arms, but I don't let go.

Not until I wake up.

I open my eyes slowly, waiting for the intense heat to disappear, but it doesn't. The body that I'm wrapped around is just as hot as the one from my nightmare.

"Wes?" I sit up and take in the scene before me.

Carter's bedroom in the light of day is even more depressing than it was last night. His open closet is full of athletic equipment and basketball trophies and a tangle of wire coat hangers. His empty dresser drawers are pulled open at random lengths like a sideways city skyline. And the man I slept with on Carter's bare mattress is curled up beside me in the fetal position, shivering and sweating and running from his own horsemen.

My eyes roam over Wes's naked body. His furrowed forehead is covered in tiny beads of moisture, his strong body is shivering despite the heat waves radiating off of it, and his bullet wound is on full display in all its gory, oozy glory.

Shit!

I was supposed to keep it clean and bandaged, but just like everything else, I forgot.

Yesterday just disappeared so quickly, I try to explain to myself. *Everything was crazy with the flat tire and the storm and being in this house and ...*

I feel my cheeks heat and the corners of my mouth curl upward as I remember what else we did yesterday. The way Wes kissed me like I was his last meal. The way he held me and called it *perfect.* The way he poured himself into me, filling the emptiness that I'd once thought was bottomless. Wes showed me depths I hadn't known he possessed last night, and I drowned in them, happily.

Wesson.

My smile widens at the thought of his name. I don't want to feel happy about what I did. What *we* did. I want to feel guilty and terrible and disgusting. I just cheated on the only boy I'd ever loved ... or thought I loved ... in his own bed, for God's sake, but ... in the words of Wesson Patrick Parker ...

Fuck 'em.

Carter left me here to die.

Wes is the only thing that makes me not want to.

I slide off the bed and sit cross-legged on the floor next to my backpack. I quietly dig past the food and water until I find the first aid kit I packed. There's plenty of ointment and bandages in there, but Wes needs antibiotics and probably some painkillers. That gory mess looks like it probably hurts a hell of a lot worse than he's been letting on.

I pull the orange prescription bottle out of the front pocket of my backpack where I stashed it while I was changing out of my wet clothes. Holding it up to the light, I'm surprised to see how many pills I have left. Thinking back, I realize that I haven't taken a single one since yesterday afternoon. I haven't needed to. Wes's kisses are my new memory-erasing drug, and if I'm really lucky—which I'm not—those won't run out.

I set the hydrocodone next to the first aid kit and tiptoe down the hall. I don't know why I feel the need to be so quiet. Maybe it's because I don't want to wake Wes up. Or maybe it's because I've spent the last few years trying to *avoid* being caught naked in Carter Renshaw's house.

I glance at the fireplace on my way through the kitchen, suddenly remembering that we left it burning before bed. But the blaze is long gone, the glass doors shut tight. I smile and shake my head. *Wes the survivalist.* I should have known he would come back out here in the middle of the night to take care of it.

Evidently, Boy Scout duty wasn't the only thing Wes was up to last night. I head toward the kitchen on my way to the laundry room but do a double take when I realize that our clothes have been laid out all over the couches and tables and floor in front of the fireplace. I remember the power outage and giggle, picturing a very naked Wes pulling our wet clothes out of the washing machine and cursing up a storm when he figured out that the dryer wouldn't work.

I pull on the plaid flannel shirt and ripped black jeans I packed for today, pleasantly surprised at how dry they are, and fold the rest of our clothes into a nice little stack—with Wes's Hawaiian shirt on top, of course.

Hugging the stiff, wrinkled cotton to my chest, I scurry through the house, opening the blinds for light and checking the bathrooms for leftover antibiotics, which I find in practically every drawer and medicine cabinet I check.

"If April 23 doesn't kill us all, antibiotic resistance will. Now, take those."

I chuckle as my mom's smart-ass comment from months ago surfaces in the recesses of my mind. I was recovering from a sinus infection, and she made sure I took every last damn antibiotic I'd been prescribed. She even watched me swallow them like a prison nurse.

Sudden awareness slaps the amused smirk right off my face.

A memory. Shit.

Pushing it away, I toss a fourth unfinished prescription bottle onto my stack of clothes and step into the master bathtub to open the blinds. The sliver of sky I see above the pines is still angry and gray, but it's stopped raining. I focus on that tiny miracle. On the glimmer of hope that we might find the shelter today.

We have to find it today.

All we have left is today.

When I turn to go check on Wes, a scream bursts out of me. Pill bottles tumble into the bathtub, rattling like handfuls of gravel against the porcelain.

"Fuck," I gasp, clutching the folded bundle to my chest. "You scared the shit outta me!"

The tall, muscular, tattooed man blocking my exit leans his uninjured shoulder against the doorframe. "You scared me first."

He's completely unashamed of his nudity, but I'm too concerned about his pale, clammy face and bluish, heavy eyelids to appreciate the view.

"One of the horsemen took you from me. Pulled you right out of my arms, and ..." His voice trails off and he shakes his head, ridding himself of whatever torturous fate I just suffered in his mind. "When I woke up, you were gone."

"I'm sorry." I frown, setting the pile of clothes on the edge of the tub.

I walk over and wrap my arms around the sweet, sleepy, naked man. Wes pulls me in and kisses the top of my head, and I'm reminded how warm he is. Too warm.

"I went to find you some antibiotics," I mutter into his bare chest.

His skin is damp and smells like sweat.

"I let your bullet wound get infected." I feel the weight of guilt settle over me, pressing me into the floor as I say the words out loud. "I'm so sorry, Wes. I'll take better care of it, I promise. Look"—I let go of him and head toward the bathtub, eager to get away from the disappointed look that I'm sure he's giving me right now—"I found you some medicine."

"Is that why I feel like shit? I thought it was just the vodka." Wes's joke lands on me like a slap of shame.

"Yeah, that's why you feel like shit."

My guts twist as I gather the bottles in my hands and scan their labels. There are two prescriptions of Keflex that, together, might make close to a whole round. I walk over to the counter and busy myself with combining the pills into one container, reading the dosing instructions—anything to keep from looking at Wes.

Instead, I find myself looking into the open, lifeless eyes of the two guys who shot at him. An image of them lying on the ground flashes before me, as clear and gruesome as a crime scene photo. Their slack facial muscles, the red mess, the glass everywhere. I killed them. I killed two people less than forty-eight hours ago, and I haven't even thought about them since. I wince and squeeze my eyes shut, gripping the edge of the counter until the vault finally does its job and swallows the memory back down.

I should be relieved, but I'm not. My heart begins to sputter, and my palms begin to sweat. That was two memories in less than ten minutes.

What if more come? What if—

I need to take another pill. I need to take two. I can't do this …

I vaguely register the sight of Wes's naked form coming to stand next to me as I stare through the mirror over the sink.

"You okay?"

Righting myself, I pull on a fake grin and glance up at the reflection of his pale face. "Yeah." I shake a white tablet into my hand and offer it to him. "Just take one of these every six hours until they're"—Wes pops the medicine into his mouth and swallows before I've even finished my sentence—"gone. I, uh, have some antibiotic ointment, too, and bandages, but we need to clean your wound first."

I feel Wes staring at me as my eyes dart around the bathroom, looking for a diversion. I feel the heat radiating off his body, trying to fight the infection I caused. And I feel the question on his lips before he speaks it.

My armpits start to sweat.

Great. Now, we're both sweating.

A shower. We need to shower.

I run over to the shower and turn on the faucet.

"I'll just clean your wound in here," I call over my shoulder. "It'll be easier this way and we might as well take advantage of the hot water before the gas gets cut off and the bomb shelter probably doesn't have running water at all ..." I'm rambling. I can hear myself talking a mile a minute, but there's nothing I can do about it. I can't even look at him.

He'll know. He'll see all my secrets, and he'll just *know*. I can't let that happen. He said it himself; people leave when they figure out how fucked up you are, and I need him to stay. I need him to distract me. I need him to get better ...

I undo the top two buttons on my flannel before my hands start to shake, and I just yank the whole thing off over my head. My bra puts up even more of a fight. I can feel Wes watching me as I struggle with the clasp.

"Hey," he says, his voice as soft and cautious as his footsteps as he crosses the bathroom to help.

Once he reaches me, I drop my hands in defeat and let him unfasten it, concentrating on the way his fingertips feel against my skin.

"Breathe, okay?" he whispers, guiding my opened bra down my arms and onto the floor at my feet. "Just breathe."

I do as he said, inhaling the steamy air through my nose until my lungs can't hold anymore. My whole body sags as I exhale.

Wes's hands grip the muscles on either side of my neck and squeeze, almost to the point of pain, before releasing and moving a few inches down to my shoulders. He squeezes and releases again, moving down to my biceps. By the time his hands are at my wrists, I'm a limp noodle, leaning backward against his hot, clammy chest.

"You're thinking about what happened at the grocery store, aren't you?"

I nod even though that's just the tip of the iceberg. Just a pebble tossed on top of the mountain of shit I'm trying to keep submerged.

"Well, don't. You saved my life by taking those guys out, and now, you're doing it all over again with this." Wes sweeps his hand over to the cluster of orange bottles on the counter behind us.

Dropping his chapped lips to my bare shoulder, he reaches in front of me to unbutton my jeans. Wes slides my pants and panties down my legs as I splay my trembling hands on the steamy shower door and step out of them.

Standing back up, Wes wraps his arms around me from behind. His erection nuzzles into the crease of my ass, but his embrace doesn't feel sexual. It feels like he's trying to hold me together.

"Why are you doing all this for me?"

My stomach churns out a fresh batch of acid as my heart begins to pound through my back against Wes's chest.

How do I answer that without sounding even crazier than he already suspects that I am?

Because I think I might be in love with you.

Because, before I met you, I hadn't smiled in a month.

Because I don't want to lose you.

Because you're my only reason for living.

"Look at me."

I hold my breath as Wes turns my body around to face him. Then, with a swallow, I lift my head and accept my fate. I let him see me in all my naked, bruised, fucked up glory. Even sick, Wes's beauty takes my breath away. His pale green eyes are rimmed in red—tired and determined, hopeless and hopeful. His dark eyebrows pull together as he chews on the inside of his bottom lip. He's looking at me like I'm a precious puzzle, and everything else fades away. More than the pills or the memories or the fear of what tomorrow will bring, I realize that I am a slave to that *look*. I would do anything, give *anything*, to spend what's left of my short life watching Wes watching me.

He asks his question again, "Why are you doing this, Rain? Why are you taking care of me?"

"Because ... I like taking care of people?" It's not a lie. "I was gonna start nursing school last fall, but then, you know, everything went to shit. But, seeing as how I can't even keep my first patient from getting an infection, it's probably for the best."

I attempt a smile, but Wes doesn't return it. His intense, bloodshot eyes dart back and forth between mine while he makes up his mind about me. Then, he nods.

"What?" My cheeks suddenly feel as if I'm the one with the fever.

"Nothing. Come on. Shower's hot."

I blink, and Wes is gone, replaced with a plume of steam from the opening and closing of the shower door.

I follow him in and freeze at the sight of his head thrown back under the spray. Rivulets of warm water crisscross over his chest and slide into the valleys between his abs. Wes is no more than a foot away from me, but I feel as though I couldn't touch him even if I wanted to. He's shut me out, and I don't even know why.

I feel like, if things were normal right now, this is the part where Wes would tell me he'd call me on his way out the door, never to be heard from again.

I don't know what I did, but I messed up. I gave the wrong answer, and now, I'm being shunned for it.

"Wes." My wavering, raspy voice is almost completely drowned out by the roar of the shower. I clear my throat and continue, a little louder, "Wes."

He turns to look at me but flinches and curses under his breath as the hard spray lands directly on his gaping wound.

Without thinking, I reach out and cup my hands above the gash, shielding it from the onslaught. "Just stand here for a minute," I say, angling him so that the water hits his back and runs down his arm, cleaning out the injury without all the blunt force trauma.

Wes jerks his shoulder, pulling his arm out of my hand. "I can take it from here. You're off the clock, *Nurse Williams*." He says it like an insult. I feel it land in my gut like a sucker punch.

"Are you mad at me?"

"Nope."

I glance up and notice immediately that the hopefulness I saw just a few minutes ago has been replaced with a cement wall, painted green and lined with spiky black lashes like razor wire.

"I just don't wanna be your little *patient*, okay? I can take care of myself. I've been doing it my whole life."

And there it is.

"I've been doing it my whole life."

Nobody has ever taken care of Wes before. Not because they genuinely wanted to. Not because they cared.

"I care." My eyes go wide as my own words hit my ears. I glance up at Wes in a panic, wondering if he heard me, too. Praying to God that he didn't.

Wes stills, his bottom lip curled inward slightly as if he's just about to start chewing on it. Blood pounds in my ears louder than the water drumming on his skin as I wait for him to react, but he doesn't so much as blink.

Fuck.

A subtle hardness makes its way into the edges and angles of Wes's face. His eyes narrow, just a bit. His jaw flexes. His nostrils flare. I can't tell what he's fighting back, but whatever it is, it scares me.

"Listen to me," he grinds out from between his clenched teeth. "I'm not your fucking boyfriend, okay? I'm the guy who put a gun to your head two days ago. Remember? You don't know me, you don't fucking love me, and you never will. So, stop ..." Wes shakes his head and glances around the inside of the shower, hunting for the words he needs in the swirling mist. "Stop ... *this*. Stop pretending like you give a shit."

His accusation makes me livid.

"Stop pretending like I don't!" I shout, balling my hands into fists at my sides as the emotion I've been trying to hide from him bubbles up and boils to the surface. "Stop pretending like you're this unlovable monster when you're the boldest, bravest, most ... most beautiful person I've ever met!" My fingernails dig into my palms as fury surges through my body. "And stop pretending like I'm only here because you kidnapped me. You didn't kidnap me, and you know it. You saved me, Wes. And every time you look at me, you do it all over again!"

It happens at once, but the first thing I register is Wes's lips on my lips. His kiss is needy and desperate and tastes like my tears. I feel his hands clutching the back of my head next. Then, I begin to process the cold, hard tiles against my back. He's kissing me like he did at the hardware store when he realized that we weren't going to get shot—up against the shelves, angry and relieved and unable to express it any other way.

But, this time, there are no clothes between us, no hang-ups or reservations, and no storm brewing outside. This time, when I hitch my thigh over the V of his hip, he's able to slide against me without a barrier. This time, when I angle myself so that he's lined up perfectly, he fills me until my back drags up the wall, and my toes barely touch the ground. This time, I feel him everywhere. His feverish skin warms me from the outside in. His palms glide over my wet curves like he's molding them from clay. And his heart—I feel that too—is pounding away just as hard as mine.

This connection is more intense than anything I've ever experienced. It's as if he becomes someone else when we touch. No, it's as if he becomes *himself*. The real Wesson. The one who is loving and passionate and aching for affection. I cling to that version as he takes me higher, pressing me into the wall and wrapping my other thigh around his waist. His strength is the only thing keeping me from falling, in more ways than one, and when I feel him swell inside of me, so does my heart.

I tighten my legs around his waist and pull him even closer, wanting as much of him as I can get. And he gives it to me, driving forward until his body rocks against my sensitive flesh, triggering an explosion of convulsions between my legs and fireworks behind my eyes. Wes follows me over the edge, groaning against my lips as his pulsing, jerking surge of heat fills me deep and makes me glow.

I don't remember how long it's been since my last birth control shot, and honestly, I don't care. The only thing that matters right now is that, if I die tomorrow—and I very well might—it will be with a smile on my face and Wesson Patrick Parker by my side.

CHAPTER 17

Wes

I SUCK A BREATH in through my nose and exhale through my gritted teeth as I sit on the edge of Fuckface's bed and let Rain play doctor with my bullet wound.

She wrinkles her forehead and gives me an apologetic look. "Sorry, I know it hurts. I'm almost done."

It's not the gaping hole in my arm that hurts; it's the one in my fucking soul that has me looking around for something to bite down on. The one that wants to shove Rain across the room and scream at her to stop touching me like that. It's the part of me that's never had somebody kiss my stupid fucking boo-boos that wants to rip the bandage out of her hand and slap it on myself. This shit is unbearable.

"There you go." She smiles, sealing the edges of the bandage down with gentle fingers.

I catch her leaning in with her fat pink lips pursed, but I jump to my feet before she can actually kiss it. She might as well stab me in the fucking heart. Every kind thing Rain does for me is just one more reminder of everything I've been missing my whole fucking life. And, honestly, I'd rather not know.

I was so much happier when people used me for a paycheck from the government or a fuck boy, and I used them for a roof over my head or a place to stick my dick. I knew where I stood. Things were simple, relationships were temporary, and I knew all the rules. Hell, I'd invented them.

But this shit with Rain is fucking with my head. I don't know what's real anymore. I don't know if she actually cares about me or if she's just using me as a stand-in for her missing boyfriend. I don't know if I'm keeping her around because she's useful or if I've gone and done the one thing I swore I would never do to another person as long as I lived.

Gotten attached.

I feel Rain watching me as I pace the floor of her *real* boyfriend's bedroom like a caged animal. "We've gotta go." I don't have to tell her why. Tomorrow's date is hanging over our heads like the blade of a guillotine.

Rain nods once. She looks younger today without all that makeup on. Her wet hair hangs limp around her face and stops bluntly at her chin. The sleeves of her plaid flannel shirt are too long and bunched in her fists. And her wide blue eyes blink up at me with the trusting innocence of a child.

This isn't just about me anymore, and that fact makes finding the bomb shelter even more imperative.

I pull my holster on over my wifebeater and cover it with my Hawaiian shirt. I couldn't sleep last night until I got my gun from the kitchen. I can't ever sleep unless I know there's a weapon within arm's reach. Even as a kid, I used to stash a kitchen knife under my pillow at night.

I wish I could say I'd never had to use it.

Rain slides off the bed and kneels beside the backpack while I pull on my jeans and boots. She shoves her extra clothes, the first aid kit, and my meds inside, but not the hydrocodone. That she uncaps and shakes into her palm without making a sound. I watch out of the corner of my eye as she covertly pushes a little white pill into her mouth and tucks the orange bottle into her bra through the neck of her shirt.

At first, I thought she didn't want me to see her dosing because she was afraid I'd take her pills again, but the more I watch her, the more I realize she's not afraid; she's ashamed. She's ashamed of her dependence.

I know the fucking feeling.

Crash!

The sound of glass breaking down the hall shatters our silence. Rain and I freeze, our eyes locking as a chorus of giggles and curse words echo through the house.

"See? I told you they left." A girl's voice.

"Damn. I was really hoping I'd get to fuck Carter Renshaw before I died." Another girl.

"We all were, honey." A guy.

Their laughter fills the house as the color drains from Rain's face.

"You know them?" I whisper.

Rain simply nods and covers her mouth with her sleeves.

"I don't know why the hell he wasted all his time with *Rainbow Williams.*" The way this bitch says her name makes me wish she were a guy so that I could go out there and bash her face in.

"Uh … 'cause she's gorgeous," the guy replies, lisping a little on the last S.

I want to bash his face in, too.

"I guess, if you're into that whole goody-goody, Little Miss Perfect thing. But Carter was captain of the basketball team. He should have been dating a cheerleader."

Rain's eyes drop to the floor, and I see red.

"Oh, like you?" the other girl sasses back.

"Yeah. Duh."

I hear cabinet doors opening and shutting as the trio continues their shit-talking in the kitchen. With the bedroom door wide open and no other sound in the house, we can still hear them clearly. *Too* clearly.

"Well, *I* made out with him senior year, so maybe he just had a thing for blondes."

Rain's eyes flick to mine, wide with shock.

"Oh my God, you little slut!" the cheerleader cackles. "I can't believe you never told me!"

"Are you serious? You would have told the whole school by Monday, and Rainbow probably would have killed herself by Tuesday."

"Ugh, you're so right."

I watch Rain shrink, disappearing into her flannel shirt until only her flushed pink face is visible.

"For real. After we kissed, Carter actually told me he wanted to break up with her, but he was afraid it would, like, send her over the edge. She always seemed so depressed, you know?"

"Oh, I know. And then she dyed her hair black and started wearing that awful hoodie. I wanted to be like, *Girl, I know the world's ending and all, but you are dating Carter Renshaw. Get some highlights and cheer the fuck up.*"

My irritation flares with the mention of that fucker's hoodie but cools as soon as I realize that Rain's not wearing it today. In fact, she hasn't put any of his clothes back on since last night.

"I don't know," the guy chimes in. "I think Carter should have been on the DL with a certain fluffy queen from drama club instead. Wouldn't that have just been scandalous?"

I reach over and give Rain's thigh a squeeze. "You want me to kill 'em?" I whisper, only partly joking.

The corner of Rain's mouth lifts in a half-assed smile, but the look on her face is one hundred percent kicked puppy.

Crouching down, I look her dead in the fucking eyes and whisper, "Hey, what's our job?"

The other corner of her mouth quirks up to match the first. "To say *fuck 'em* and survive anyway?"

I smirk at my star student, feeling a swell of possessive pride fill my chest. "Very good, Miss Williams," I whisper. "Very—"

"Oh my God, you guys! Corn dogs!"

"That's it. These fuckers are gonna die."

The impulse to shoot them where they stand sends a thrill down my spine as I pull the 9-millimeter out of my holster. I let the magazine drop into my open palm and count the number of bullets left—or I should say, *bullet*.

"Fuck," I hiss, slamming the clip back into the handle.

Rain shushes me and places a finger to her lips.

I sigh and whisper the bad news, "I only have one bullet left. You're gonna have to pick the one you hate the most."

Rain giggles into her sleeves, and the sight makes my heart pound like a fucking gorilla's fist against my chest. She's nothing like the girl those bitches described. She's strong and resilient and sweet and—lucky for one of them—forgiving.

"I don't want you to kill them," she admits, looking up at me from under her naturally black lashes, a sheepish smile tugging at the corners of her mouth.

"Why not?"

"Because they just made me feel *so* much better."

Either that pill kicked in way faster than I expected or she's finally snapped.

"You feel *better*? After hearing *that*?" I gesture toward the empty hallway with my gun.

Rain nods, swallowing me whole with her expanding pupils. "If Carter cheated, then that means I don't have to feel bad anymore. About"—her eyes drop to the floor as she shrugs, but when they find mine again, they're glimmering with courage—"*us*."

Us. Fuck me.

I don't do us*!* I want to fire back, but the words die in my mouth as I realize that they're no longer true. When I look into that beautiful, hopeful, frightened face, the only thing I see is everything I've ever wanted.

Us.

From the kitchen, we hear the microwave door slam shut and a plate land with a thud on the counter. "Damn it! I forgot the power's out!"

A snort bursts out of Rain before I clap my hand over her mouth, choking on my own laughter. We tumble to the carpet, and I reach out, pushing the door almost completely shut with my hand, hoping it will muffle some of the sounds we're making.

"Guess those assholes aren't gonna get to eat your corn dogs after all," I whisper, my lips grazing her ear.

"Shh-h-h-h-h." Rain giggles even though she's the one making all the damn noise. Her body shakes underneath me with suppressed laughter as I drop my lips to her shushing mouth.

I vaguely process the sounds of shouting and squealing and banging around in the kitchen, but my senses are too busy feasting on a rainbow to pay them much attention anymore.

Rain smells different today, like fruity shampoo instead of sugar cookies, but the feel of her hasn't changed a bit. Her soft, round edges are obedient—molding to fit the shape of my cupped hands, smoothing flat against my hard planes—but her tongue is a defiant little cocktease. It coaxes me deeper just to disappear with a wet *smack* as her lips slide down the length of my tongue. The tiny, breathy noises she makes as her hips rise up to meet mine are the sexiest sounds I've ever fucking heard, and the sight of her beneath me—eyes shut, back arched, lips parted—could only be better if she were naked.

"Wes …"

That one whispered word has me ready to tear the buttons off her fucking shirt. I push up onto my forearms to do just that when her eyes pop open, wide and worried.

"Wes, do you smell smoke?"

I sit up and inhale, coughing immediately as my lungs reject the hazy gray air tumbling in from the hallway. "Fuck!"

I grab Rain by the arms and yank her to her feet, but we both start coughing as soon as we're upright. The air is so much thicker up here. So much hotter. It burns my eyes and sears my nostrils as I fight to suck the oxygen from it.

"Get down!" I command, pulling Rain to the ground as I drop to my knees. Crawling over to the door, I look down the hallway and listen for signs of life, but all I hear are the sounds of destruction coming from the kitchen.

Rain is right behind me as we make our way toward the living room, which looks like it's been inhabited by a swirling black thundercloud. A crash so loud it sounds like a stack of dishes falling off the back of a pickup truck cuts through the thickened air. I ignore it as we emerge from the hallway, my sights set on the closest exit. I turn left and head toward the front door, careful to avoid the broken glass those little shits left everywhere on their way in. When I reach the handle and throw that fucker open, I gulp two lungfuls of humid air before turning to help Rain navigate the glass.

"Rain?"

Another crash, even louder than the first, rattles the walls as I peer into the blackness, looking for my girl.

"Rain!"

"I'll be right"—*cough*—"back!" Rain's voice sounds strangled as it filters through the smog.

"What the fuck are you doing?" I scream. When I don't get a response, I barrel headfirst into the house. "Rain!"

Knowing her, she probably went to go check on those dumb fucks in the kitchen, so I charge into the living room, heading toward the source of the smoke at the back of the house. After a few feet, the air gets so thick and hot and hard to breathe that I have to drop to my elbows and army crawl the rest of the way.

"Rain!" I call one last time before making it to the entryway of the kitchen, which now resembles the fiery fucking gates of hell.

The entire back wall of cabinets is engulfed in flames. They're burning so bright and so hot it's as if they were varnished with bacon grease. The stove appears to be the source of the inferno—or I should say, the mangled, melting tower of Tupperware piled on top of the gas burners, which have been turned on full blast. The bottom has already burned out of the cabinets to the left and right of the stove, hence the crashing dishes we heard, and it looks like the roof is gonna be the next thing to give.

There's no sign of Rain or the motherfuckers who set the fire, so I turn around and crawl back the way I came.

At least, I *think* it's the way I came. The air is so black I can't see my own hand in front of my face. I stop as my coughing gets the better of me, but the sound of the ceiling buckling above propels me forward. My heart races faster with every foot of ground that I cover. I should have reached the front door by now. I should have at least hit a wall. Regret coils around my throat, stealing the air from my lungs.

"Rain!" I snarl between lungfuls of poison, her name leaving an even worse taste in my mouth than the noxious fumes I'm breathing for her.

I knew from that very first day that she was going to be the death of me. I knew it, and I let it happen anyway.

"*Us,*" I hear her soft voice coo in my head.

The sound makes me want to puke.

This is what us *gets you. It gets you fucking killed.*

I hear her voice again and assume I must be hallucinating until I realize that she's not saying *us.*

She's saying, "Wes! Wes! Oh my God!"

I feel her tiny hands reach out to me in the dark, gripping my arms, touching my face. The relief I feel that she's alive is overshadowed by the rage burning inside me hotter than a Tupperware fire.

"Just a few more feet. Watch out for the glass."

I feel something sharp cut into my forearm as the light of day becomes a gauzy reality up ahead. Rain shuffles backward out the door as I follow, tumbling onto the porch where I alternate between coughing and dry-heaving until the world finally stops spinning. All the while, I can feel her concerned hands all over me.

"Fucking stop!" I yell, swatting her away as I crawl over to the edge of the porch. I hack up something black and spit it into the bushes below. My head is pounding, and my heart is too as I try to figure out what the fuck to say to her.

"I'm so sorry." Her voice is a trembling whisper as she sits on the porch next to where my head is hanging over the ledge. "I just ran back to the bedroom real quick to get the backpack. All your medicine was in there. I couldn't just leave it. But, when I got back, you were gone. I ran around the whole house looking for you before I realized you'd gone back inside."

Her story soothes my anger a little bit but not the festering truth gnawing away at the pit of my stomach—the truth that love and survival are mutually exclusive in my world. I allowed myself to think, for just a few hours, that maybe this time would be different. Maybe I would finally get to have both. Maybe God doesn't fucking hate me.

"Wes, say something. Please."

"We should get off the porch."

Rain jumps to her feet and reaches out to help me up, but I wave her off and use the railing to pull myself up. Stumbling down the stairs, I look for the sun, trying to figure out what time it is. I can't even find it through the plume of black smoke billowing into the sky above the house, but based on the way the trees' shadows are clinging to the right side of their trunks, I'd say it's already after noon.

Fuck.

Once again, I find myself tempted to tell her to go home. To scream it at her, but when I turn to deliver the blow, I just can't. Rain's forehead is wrinkled in concern. Her blue eyes are rounded in remorse. And when she blinks, twin tears sparkle in the sunlight as they slide down her cheeks.

"Come here," I demand, feeling my chest swell and crack and splinter as she leaps forward and buries herself in it.

"I was so scared," she wails, fisting the back of my shirt as sobs rack her body. "I thought … I thought I'd lost you!"

I run my hand over her hair as her words pierce my heart like daggers, the pain more intense than my bullet wound or my soot-stained lungs.

I've finally found what I've been missing my whole life, and if I keep it, it will kill me.

No wonder Rain was wearing a black hoodie when I met her.

She's the fifth fucking horseman of the apocalypse.

CHAPTER 18

Rain

HEAT SCORCHES MY BACK as the house goes up in flames behind me, but I can't let go of Wes. Not yet.

Two nights ago, I had a nightmare about Burger Palace, and the next morning I got attacked inside of one. Last night, I had a dream that we burned in a fire, and it almost happened a few hours later. What if these aren't just coincidences? What if the nightmares are coming true?

I remember what Wes said about dreaming that I was taken away from him last night, and my fists curl into his shirt.

The sound of a bomb going off behind me pulls a scream from my lungs. I bury my face in Wes's shirt and feel his hand cover the back of my head. I try to relax, but his grip is too hard. His posture too rigid.

"What was that?" I ask without looking up, hoping it was just the stove exploding or the roof caving in.

When Wes doesn't answer right away, I glance up at his jaw, tight and grinding. His eyes cut to mine, and his chest puffs up beneath my cheek.

Exhaling through his flared nostrils, Wes finally replies, "My bike."

We walk around the side of Carter's burning house, and sure enough, Wes was right. He'd parked his bike right against the house, next to the back door, and when the fire finally chewed through the kitchen wall, Wes's gas tank got so hot that it exploded.

As we walk past the debris on our way toward the trail—a handlebar here, a fender there—the only thing I can think of to say is, "I'm sorry."

"It's fine," he says without looking at me. "I don't need it anymore anyway." His curt response gives me chills. It's detached and automatic, like he's said it a million times to rationalize a million different losses.

"I don't need it anymore anyway."

Will he feel that way when the horsemen take me from him, too?

This morning, he wouldn't have. This morning, he said the nightmare scared him, that waking up without me *scared* him. But now, I don't know. It's like the real Wes died in that fire, and all I got back is the outer shell.

We're silent as we enter the woods and begin our walk down the trail, concentrating on avoiding the mud puddles and fallen branches in our path.

"I guess it's a good thing we're not on the bike," I say, stepping over the trunk of a fallen pine tree. "This trail is a mess."

"Yeah," Wes deadpans, clearing the obstacle without even looking down.

His eyes are fixed on something up ahead. I follow his gaze and feel my already-heavy heart sink even more. Wes is staring at the side of my tree house.

"Did you go see your mom last night?"

"Uh ... no," I stammer, stepping over another fallen tree. "I ... went early this morning, before you woke up."

Wes nods slowly, pressing his lips together in a hard line as his eyes drop to my hiking boots. The hiking boots he probably saw on Carter's bedroom floor when he woke up.

Right where I'd left them the night before.

My sinking heart goes into a full-on free fall at the realization that Wes knows I'm lying, but that's the only sensation the drugs allow me to feel. I don't look at my house at all as we pass. It's not there. It doesn't exist. Nothing exists, except for my feet on this trail. No past. No future. No feelings. No fear. Just the *squish, squish, splash* of mud beneath my boots and the sound of birds busily rebuilding their nests after the storm.

I breathe the cool, humid air and sigh. With the gray clouds overhead and the woodsy smell of burning leaves on the breeze, it feels more like fall than spring.

But people don't burn leaves in the spring.

Looking around, I notice a plume of smoke rising above the trees up ahead. I wonder if we got turned around somehow and are actually headed back toward Carter's house. This doesn't smell like Carter's fire though—all that melting plastic and wood varnish. This fire smells cozy and delicious.

Wes doesn't seem to appreciate the scent as much as I do. As we get closer, his cough gets worse. I guess his poisoned lungs have had enough smoke inhalation for one day. Pulling his shirt over his nose, Wes lets a yellow hibiscus filter his oxygen as we press on, emerging from the woods behind the raging inferno that was once the Franklin Springs public library.

"I guess the orgy got a little out of hand," Wes muses between coughs as we round the side of the building.

When I realize that the homey smell I was enjoying is actually the scent of burning books, something like sadness begins to settle around me, but the hydrocodone tosses it off like an unwanted blanket.

Wes coughs into his shirt as we cross the street, hacking something up and spitting it onto the littered asphalt. He's so pale. His lips are almost bluish, and the sweaty sheen from this morning is back.

"You okay?" I ask as soon as we step into the Burger Palace parking lot, but Wes doesn't seem to hear me.

His eyes are trained on the thirty-foot-tall digital billboard overhead. "How the fuck is that sign on if the power's out?" he mutters.

"They probably have a generator for it." I roll my eyes. "God forbid we have to go a day without seeing stupid King Burger on his stupid fucking horse."

Horse.

I eye the flashing multicolored image of King Burger on his trusty steed, Mister Nugget, as we pass below. He's holding his French fry staff in the air like a sword—or a mace or a scythe or a flaming club—and a nagging sense of déjà vu tugs at the edges of my fuzzy consciousness.

The sound of gunfire inside the restaurant chases it away.

Wes grabs my hand and takes off running toward the woods as people come pouring out of every exit, screaming and shrieking and calling out the names of their loved ones.

Some of whom I've known my whole life.

"*Fuck 'em,*" Wes's voice says inside my head as the *splish, splish, splash* of mud beneath my feet returns.

Fuck 'em, I repeat, this time in my own voice.

I don't look back, and I don't let go. I run hand in hand with this beautiful stranger, over roots and beneath branches, feeling more alive than I ever have.

Wes, on the other hand …

When we finally make it back to the place we were searching yesterday, he doubles over and places his hands on his knees, coughing and hacking until his face goes from ashen to purple.

I struggle to yank the backpack off his stubborn, hunched-over shoulders and push him to sit on the fallen log we rested on yesterday. I pull a bottle of water out of the bag and hand it to him. Wes chugs almost the whole thing before taking a breath.

Reaching into the neck of my shirt, I pull the little orange bottle out of my bra and unscrew the cap. "Here," I sigh, shaking one of my few remaining painkillers into my palm. "This'll make you feel better."

"I don't want to fucking feel better," Wes snaps, shoving my hand away.

I gasp as the tiny, precious tablet goes flying, disappearing a few feet away in a fat bed of wet pine needles.

"I want to find that goddamn bomb shelter!"

Ignoring my shocked expression, Wes shoves his arm elbow deep into the backpack next to me, rooting around until he finds the giant magnets in the bottom. "The *only* thing that's gonna make me feel better is being in a cement bunker underground before midnight." Wes shoves one of the homemade metal detectors in my direction. "Come on."

I accept the magnet with a frown. "Will you at least eat something first?"

"I'll eat when I find the fucking shelter!" he yells, pushing to his feet. "I'll rest when I find the fucking shelter. I'll take your pills—"

"When you find the fucking shelter. Okay, I get it." I nod, blinking back startled tears.

"Do you?" he snaps, tossing the magnet on the ground in front of his muddy boots and pulling the rope taut. "Because I feel like all you've done since we met is sidetrack me and try to get me killed."

"I know," I mumble, my eyes drifting over to the place where my pill disappeared. I could really use it right about now. Standing, I wander over to the mound of pine needles, hoping to find a glimmer of white in all that brown. I stare down at the crisscrossing lines on the ground, a chaotic pattern as pointless as my short, stupid life.

I'm sorry, I want to say. *I was just trying to help,* I think to myself. *You're better off without me.*

But the words don't come out of my mouth.

I'm too distracted by the shape of the mound in front of me. Bending over, I shove my hands into the wet pine straw, but they don't disappear into the mulchy mess like they should. Instead, my fingertips jam into something large and hard just below the surface. When I brush the needles away, my mouth falls open at the sight of a large stone block ... attached to another stone block with crumbling white mortar.

"Wes!" I shout, frantically uncovering the chain of stones. "Wes, I found it! I found the chimney!"

A split second later, Wes is at my side, kissing my temple and apologizing profusely as we work together to unearth the fallen chimney. Once we locate the base, he knows exactly where to look for the hatch. He turns and takes about ten steps away, like a pirate measuring paces on a treasure map, and then he drops the magnet. This time, there's no bounce when it lands on the soft forest floor. Hopeful green eyes lock on to mine as Wes tugs on the rope. The metal disc doesn't budge.

I stand, rooted to the spot, as he falls to his knees and begins clawing at the carpet of leaves and needles beside the magnet. As the surface of a rusted metal door begins to take shape under his determined hands, I feel as if he's lifting a weight off of me as well.

We're going to be okay.
I was helpful.
Wes will be happy with me again.

"Shit," he hisses, uncovering a rusty old padlock secured to the side of the door. Giving it a tug, Wes drops it with a clang against the door. Bracing his hands on his thighs, he furrows his brow at the new challenge, as if he were trying to unlock it with the sheer force of his mind. After a moment, he nods. Then, he reaches into the side of his open shirt and pulls the 9-millimeter out of his holster. "Go stand behind that tree. I'm gonna shoot the lock off, and I don't want you to get hit by the ricochet."

With a nod, I scurry behind the nearest oak tree and feel my heart pound as I wait for the shot to ring out. I should be excited, but this sensation fighting through the drugs feels closer to dread. This is our last bullet.

What if he misses? What if he gets hit by the ricochet? What if—

The sudden blast rattles my eardrums as it crashes and echoes off the trees. When I open my eyes and lower my hands from my ears, I wait for confirmation that it's safe to come out, but all I hear is the exaggerated *squeeeeeeak* of a metal door being opened.

Then, nothing.

With a deep breath, I peek around the trunk of the tree. Wes is on his knees, soft brown hair hiding his face, white knuckles curled around the edge of the open doorway. He did it. He fucking did it. And with hours to spare. Wes should be running around, shouting in triumph, but instead, he looks like he's kneeling before the executioner. I can't figure out why until I look into the void.

And see his tortured face staring back.

CHAPTER 19

*W*es

WATER.

The entire ... fucking ... bomb shelter ...

Is filled with water.

When I threw open that door, I didn't see salvation. I saw the happiness drain from my own eyes. I saw the smile rot off my own fucking face. In my reflection, I saw myself for what I'd always been—helpless, hopeless, powerless.

Nothing.

I have nothing. I've accomplished nothing. I've survived a lifetime of hell for nothing. And tomorrow, I'm going to return to nothing, just like everybody else. I'm not special. I'm not a survivor. I'm a fucking sham.

"Go home, Rain," I say, closing my eyes. It's bad enough that I have to hear the words coming out of my mouth. I don't want to have to see them, too.

"Wes." Her tiny voice is almost a whisper as the straw rustles beneath her approaching feet.

I hold my hand out, as if that will keep her from coming any closer. "Just ... go home. Go be with your parents."

"I don't want to," she whines. "I want to stay here. With you."

I lift my head as anger surges through my bloodstream. "You only have a few hours left to live, and you're gonna waste them on somebody you don't even know? What the fuck is wrong with you? I have nothing to offer you. No supplies, no shelter, no fucking means of self-defense!" I throw the gun in my hand as hard as I can past Rain and into the forest. "I can't save you. I can't even save myself. Go the fuck home and be with your family while you still have one."

Rain doesn't even turn her head as the weapon sails by. Her pleading, glistening eyes are trained on me and me alone. "I don't care about any of that, Wes. I ... I care about *you*."

"Well, you shouldn't," I snarl, gritting my teeth as I prepare to break what's left of my own sputtering heart. "I was just using you to help me get what I wanted, and here it is, in all its flooded glory." I sweep a hand over the cesspool in front of me and let out a disgusted laugh. "So go the fuck home, Rain. I don't need you anymore."

The lie tastes like arsenic on my tongue and hits Rain with a force almost as deadly. Her mouth drops open, and her eyes blink rapidly as she struggles to process the poison I just spat at her. I expect her to argue with me. To come back with more teenage girl whining about whatever it is she *thinks* she feels for me. But she doesn't.

She swallows.

She nods.

She tucks her head to hide her quivering chin.

And then she says the words that cut deeper than any goodbye I've ever suffered through.

"I just wanted to help."

CHAPTER 20

Rain

MY FEET FEEL LIKE cinder blocks as I stumble back down the trail toward the highway, struggling to open the childproof bottle in my shaking hands.

Don't fucking cry.

Don't you dare fucking cry.

My eyes, my throat, my lungs—they burn worse than when I was crawling through Carter's smoke-filled house. But I have to hold back the tears. I have to. If I cry for *him*, then I'll have to cry for all of them. And I can't do that. I won't.

"Go home, Rain."

I look behind me, but Wes isn't following. The only thing I have left of him is his cruel, dismissive voice. I walk faster, trying to get away from it.

"Go be with your parents."

He told me he would use me up. That I would leave him. I didn't believe it at the time, but all it took was five simple words for him to prove himself right.

"I don't need you anymore."

With a desperate grunt, I rip the cap off and throw it as hard as I can against a tree. I don't look to see where it lands. It doesn't matter anymore. Nothing does.

Wes was my only hope. My only shot at life after April 23. Without him, my hours are numbered.

Without him, I don't want the ones I have left.

CHAPTER 21

Wes

AS I LISTEN TO RAIN'S footsteps getting farther away, I feel a pure, unbridled hatred begin to fester in my soul. I don't hate the nightmares or the flooded shelter or even Rain for doing exactly what I told her to. I hate the man staring back at me. I want to wrap my fucking hands around his neck and squeeze until I have the pleasure of watching all the life drain from his eyes. Because he's the one who made her leave.

He's the one who makes everyone leave.

His fucking face is nothing more than a lie. He uses it to trick people into thinking he's trustworthy. Attractive. Confident. Strong. But he's an ugly, lying piece of shit that people can't wait to get away from as soon as they see past the facade.

I spit in his worthless fucking face, watching it distort into ripples just before I slam the metal door with a primal scream.

The clang vibrates through my arms and into my chest and rattles a cough from my smoke-stained lungs. When the silence falls back around me, it comes with a strange sense of calm.

The man is gone.

I don't know who I am without him, but I feel lighter. Younger. Freer. I no longer have anything to fear because every bad thing that could possibly happen to me has already happened. Because of him.

And, now, he's locked away for good.

I pick up Rain's backpack, noting how heavy it is. As my feet begin to move, my strides feel too long. My point of view unusually high. I'm a kid again, in a grown-up's body, walking home with a backpack full of food scored from the dumpster behind Burger Palace like I did every afternoon.

The trail is wider than I remember. Muddier, too. But the birds are singing the same songs they always have, and the trees smell just as piney. I almost expect Mama and Lily to be waiting for me when I get home. Mama will probably be passed out on the couch with that thing in her arm or arguing with her "friend" in the bedroom. Lily will probably be screaming in her crib. Her little face will light up when I walk in the room, but she'll start crying again after a minute or two. Mama said babies do that. They just "cry all the damn time."

When I cut through the Garrisons' backyard, I notice that their swing set is gone. I used to spend hours playing on that thing with their son, Benji. The Patels' house, next door, looks like it hasn't been lived in for years. The grass comes past my knees, and a few windows are broken out. Junk cars line the road, which is littered with broken television sets, glass vases, dishes—anything that the big kids might like to smash. I let my feet carry me across the destruction, but with every crunch of my boots, it becomes more and more apparent that the squat beige house at the end of the street isn't my home anymore.

And it hasn't been for a long, long time.

"Four-five-seven Prior Street," I told the woman on the phone when I called 911 like they'd taught me at school.

"What's your emergency?"

"My baby sister stopped crying."

"Son, is this a prank phone call?"

"No, ma'am. She ... she won't wake up. She's all blue, and she won't wake up."

"Where is your mommy?"

"She won't wake up either."

The mailbox still says *457*, but the house looks nothing like I remember. For starters, it's been painted—light gray with bright white trim—and the shutters, well, it has some. The rotten front steps that used to wobble when I ran down them, always on the verge of missing the bus, have been replaced, and hanging from the side of the porch, where the giant wasp's nest used to be, is a blue-and-red plastic baby swing.

My chest constricts as I instinctively listen for the sound of crying.

But there's only silence.

I run to the porch, clearing all four steps in a single leap, and press my face to one of the windows on either side of the freshly painted front door. "Hello?" I bang on the door with my fist before trying to get a better view in through one of the other windows. "Hello!" I pound on the glass with my open palm.

Even though the framed photos hanging on the wall above the couch show a family of smiling strangers, I can't help but picture my mom and my sister the way I found them that day. One passed out and dead to the world, the other ...

Before I know it, I'm grasping the sides of the doorframe and kicking the motherfucker in. Wood splinters around the deadbolt as the door swings open violently. I burst into the living room and realize immediately that the place doesn't smell like cigarette smoke and sour, spilled milk anymore. The walls inside have been painted a light gray as well, and the furniture is simple and clean.

"Hello?" I move more cautiously into the hallway, my heart chugging like a freight train.

When I peek into the first room, my old room, I don't find a mattress on the floor, surrounded by a collection of flashlights in case the power went out. I find a computer desk and two matching bookcases filled with books.

Lily's crib was in my mom's room because the extra bedroom had a padlock on it. She never told me what was in there, but now, the door is wide open.

Adrenaline pushes me forward as my eyes land on a white crib, positioned against the far wall with rays of late afternoon sunlight hitting it sideways from the window. The zoo animals hanging from the mobile watch me approach, holding their breath along with me as I relive that day with every step.

I remember the relief I felt that she'd stopped crying, followed by the realization that her skin wasn't the right color. That her open eyes were fixed on nothing. That her once-chubby cheeks were sunken, her knuckles raw from incessant chewing.

But when I look into *this* crib, it's as if I'm experiencing that day in reverse. First comes the dread and then the relief.

There is no Lily. No death. No failure. Only a fitted sheet covered in pink giraffes and gray elephants and a tiny pillow embroidered with three simple words.

You are loved.

I pick it up and read it again, blinking away the sudden, stinging tears blurring my vision.

You are loved.

I grit my teeth and try to breathe through the pain.

You are loved.

I want to throw the pillow to the ground and stomp on it, but instead, I find myself clutching it to my chest, pressing it as hard as I can against the place that aches the most. I hear the words again, repeated in my mind, and realize that the voice doing the whispering isn't my own.

It belongs to a different neglected girl. One with sad blue eyes too big for her delicate face. One who found a way to care for me, even when she wasn't being cared for herself.

One that I just threw back to the wolves.

I might not have been able to save Lily, but I'm not that same scared little boy anymore.

I'm a man now.

A man who lies.

A man who steals.

But a man who will do whatever it takes to protect his girl.

CHAPTER 22

Wes

THE ENERGY IN TOWN has escalated into a fever pitch of
desperation. The parking lot fistfights and burning buildings
and rioters smashing car windows and stray dogs snarling over
Burger Palace wrappers blur together as I power through the
anarchy with my head down. Glancing up only to note how
quickly the sun is sinking behind the trees, I walk faster.

I know April 23 won't technically be here until midnight,
but from the looks of this place, I think hell is going to show
up ahead of schedule.

As I hustle across the highway, I pass a group of shitfaced
good ole boys hanging out on the tailgate of a stranded F-250.
They have the doors open, blasting some obnoxious country
song from the truck's CD player. They don't seem to notice
me, but as soon as I get within arm's reach, one of the fuckers

reaches out and grabs my backpack. It all happens so fast. One minute, I have my sights set on the smoking shell of a library across the street, and the next, I have a forty-year-old man on the pavement with my pocketknife pressed against his throat.

His stunned, glassy eyes lift to something over my head as his buddy in the truck yells, "Mikey! Git my rifle!"

Shit.

Backpack in hand, I take off running, disappearing behind a Chevy Suburban just before three bullets pierce the hood and fender. Their laughter fades behind me as I tear past the library. The exterior walls are still intact, but the fire inside has eaten through the roof and is now shooting fifteen feet into the air. A few extremely stoned-looking Franklin Springs citizens have gathered around to watch it burn.

I hope Rain made it through here okay, I think as my feet hit the trail.

If she even went home. Fuck. What if she didn't go home?

I rack my brain for other places I should search, but nothing comes to mind. Carter's house is gone. Her friends have all left town, if she even had any. The businesses around here are either boarded up, burned down, or occupied by thugs. She has to be there. She has to.

What the hell do I say to her dad?

"Hi. I'm the guy your daughter was with while you were worried sick about her for the last two and a half days. Sorry about that."

Maybe he really is deaf. If that's the case, I won't have to say anything.

As I jog, I wonder if Rain knows sign language.

I wonder if her mom will be home.

I wonder if she even has a mom anymore.

I don't slow down, the closer I get. In fact, I pick up the pace as soon as the tree house comes into view, hurdling over the fallen oak where Rain told me she went home this morning.

Why would she lie about that? What is she hiding?

Whatever it is, I have a feeling it's inside that house.

And I just shoved her back toward it with both hands.

Fucking asshole.

An idea, a wild hope, ignites in my mind as I take the wooden ladder rungs two at a time. But, when I lift my head above the threshold of the tree house, all I find are two beanbag chairs, some protein bar wrappers, and an empty bottle of whiskey. No Rain. Just remnants from our first night together.

I look over my shoulder at her house and see it the way I saw it then. The faded gray siding. The darkened windows. It looks just as empty as it did that night, but it's not. It can't be.

I hop down and feel the impact deep in my shoulder wound. It's still throbbing, but I think my fever has gone down. I slide the backpack onto my good shoulder and dig the bottle of Keflex out of the front pocket—just another reminder of all the ways Rain tried to help me.

Popping one into my mouth, I cross the overgrown backyard with a renewed determination to find her and return the favor.

I round the corner, passing her old man's pickup truck in the driveway, and march up the weather-beaten steps to her front door. With my heart in my throat, I raise my fist to knock, but the sound coming through the broken window in the door makes my blood run cold.

It's a song.

It's a Twenty One fucking Pilots song.

"Rain?" I call through the hole in the door, hoping she'll just walk over and let me in. Like anything in my life has ever been that easy.

"Rain!" I yell louder, the artery in my neck pulsing with every second that ticks by unanswered.

The only response I get back is that singer's whiny-ass voice telling me that he can't sleep because everyone has guns for hands.

Unable to stand here any fucking longer, I reach out and turn the knob. It rotates in my hand freely.

Moving so that my body is against the wall and out of view, I yell, "I'm coming in," and nudge the door open with my foot. When the action isn't met with a spray of bullets, I take a deep breath and look around the doorframe.

Then, I immediately retreat.

Gasping for air with my back against the wooden siding, I try to process the scene inside.

A dark living room. Blinds drawn shut.

A coffee table. A couch. An old-school TV.

And a man.

Sitting in a recliner, facing the door.

With a shotgun across his lap.

And his brains splattered all over the wall behind him.

With every breath I draw, the smell becomes more and more unbearable.

The smell of death. The smell of dried blood and exposed gray matter.

The song starts over.

I pull the small flashlight from my pocket and breathe into my shirt as I tiptoe into the house. Broken glass crunches under my boots.

"Rain?" I call again, swallowing down the bile rising in my throat.

I tell myself not to look as I walk past Mr. Williams to check the kitchen, but morbid fucking curiosity gets the best of me. Swinging the flashlight in his direction, I have to clamp my teeth together so hard they almost crack to keep from puking. The entire back of his head is mushy pulp, mingling with the fluffy insides of the recliner. The streaks on the once-country-blue wall behind him have long dried to a deep rust, indicating where the bigger chunks were before they slid off and calcified on the crusty, bloodstained carpet.

I don't see an entrance wound on his bloated old face, but the blood spilling over his lower lip and into his gray beard tell me that somebody put that shotgun into his mouth before pulling the trigger.

Probably him.

The color of the blood and the stench in the fucking air also tell me that this shit did not just happen. I'd say this guy's been sitting here for ...

My guts twist, and this time, no amount of teeth-clenching will keep me from hurling all over the carpet as the last two and a half days scream by in reverse.

The drugs. The secrecy. The mood swings.

The way she refused to let me come inside the house.

The way she said he wouldn't hear her knocking, wouldn't see her at the door.

The way she came running out of here that night like she'd seen a ...

I brace myself on my knees and puke again.

Oh God.

Fuck.

He's been here this whole fucking time.

The song starts over.

And now she's in here with him.

Wiping my mouth on the back of my hand, I walk over to the stairs by the open front door. As much as I hate to trap in the smell, I kick it shut. The last thing we need is wild dogs sniffing out the body.

The beam from my flashlight leads the way as I trudge up the stairs, listening for movement, crying, *anything.* But there's nothing. Nothing but that goddamn song and the sound of my own rushing pulse as I finally reach the upstairs hallway.

Five doors.

Three closed.

Here we go.

"Rain?" I call again, but I know she won't answer. I try not to consider why as I shine my flashlight into the first open door on the right.

The sight of a black braid makes my breath catch, but I exhale in relief when I realize that it's sitting on top of an overflowing trash can. Next to a toilet. Beside a sink.

There's no one inside. It's just an empty bathroom.

A thought occurs to me as I throw open the next door and find nothing but towels and sheets.

Maybe Rain *killed the bastard. I saw her mow down two motherfuckers at Huckabee Foods like it was nothing. She could have killed him too, if it were self-defense.*

I want to believe it. I want to picture Rain as the victor in this fucked up situation. I want to find her rocking in a corner somewhere because she's batshit crazy.

Not because she's broken.

The song starts over as I approach the last door on the right.

"Rain?" I knock lightly before turning the knob, not wanting to startle whoever might be inside. "It's Wes. Can I come in?" I crack the door and brace for impact, but the only thing that hits me in the face is that same putrid smell from downstairs.

Fuck.

I pull my shirt over my nose and pray to every fucking god I can think of as I approach the lump on the bed.

Please don't let it be her. Please don't let it be her. Please, God. I know you fucking hate me, but just ... fuck. Don't let it be her.

I watch helplessly as the yellow beam from my flashlight slides up the side of a four-poster bed and across the surface of a patchwork quilt covered in flowers. The bedspread has been pulled up over the person's face—or over the place where it used to be, judging by the size and location of the maroon stain on the fabric—but I don't pull it down.

I don't need to. The blonde hair fanned out over the shredded pillow—soaked in blood as thick as tar and sprinkled with fluffy down feathers—tells me everything I need to know.

There's no saving Mrs. Williams.

I just hope I'm not too late to save her daughter.

My legs are moving and my guts are churning and my hands are gripping the flashlight like a lifeline.

Not because I'm scared.

But because now, I know exactly where she is.

The music is louder at this end of the hall, so the last room on the left has to be the one. I stomp across the carpeted corridor and twist the knob. I don't knock first. I don't wait in the hallway and push the door open from a safe distance. All of my survival instincts go out the fucking window as I burst through the last obstacle standing between me and my girl.

The first thing that registers is the smell. It isn't putrid or coppery, like the rest of the house. It's as warm and sugary as vanilla cake. I close the door behind me and breathe in like a drowning swimmer breaking the surface of the water. The familiar scent fills my lungs and lifts my spirits. Looking around the room, I find the source of the smell everywhere. Lit candles illuminate every nook and cranny in Rain's small bedroom. I turn my flashlight off and stick it back in my pocket as I take in the cozy space. Clothes and notebooks cover the floor. Bookcases filled with messily arranged paperbacks and trinkets line the left wall. A daybed and side table take up most of the right. And there, on that bed, is my very own Sleeping Beauty.

Rain is lying on her stomach on top of the covers, a vision of perfection in a house of fucking horrors.

I cross the room in two steps. The first thing I do is grab Rain's glowing cell phone off the nightstand and jam my finger against the pause symbol on the screen. I set it back down and exhale in relief as that fucking song stops, and silence settles around us.

Rain is facing the wall, so I sit on the edge of her bed and run my hand over her shiny black hair. It feels smooth beneath my palm. Smooth and real. Nothing matters outside of these four walls. The chaos, the danger, the festering death. It doesn't exist. It's just me, my sleeping angel, and a glowing, silent sense of peace.

"Rain," I whisper, leaning over to kiss her temple. But, when my lips meet her flesh, my illusion of happiness comes crashing down.

Her skin is cold. Too cold.

"Rain." I shake her shoulder and watch as her limp body jostles lifelessly.

"Fuck! Rain!" I leap to my feet and roll her toward me so that I can see her face.

And it's like looking into Lily's all over again.

Purple lips.

Purple eyelids.

Ashen skin.

I'm too late.

I'm too fucking late.

"Wake up, Rain! Come on, baby! Wake up!"

My eyes and hands search every inch of her body for a bullet wound, a slit wrist, something that would explain why she's not *fucking waking up*. But there's nothing. No blood. No injuries. It's not until I rip open her flannel shirt that I find my answer.

Or rather don't find it.

Rain's precious bottle of hydrocodone is gone.

"Goddamn it, Rain!" My voice breaks on her name like a tidal wave against a seawall as I jam my fingers against her jugular, searching for a pulse I know I won't find.

"Goddamn it," I whisper, pulling her lifeless body into my arms.

I drape her long arms over my shoulders and hug her to my chest.

"I'm so sorry." The words come out as voiceless sobs.

I grip her body tighter and bury my face in her neck. Her toes barely touch the carpet as I rock her back and forth. She used to like that. It made her feel better.

"I'm so fucking sorry."

I coil my arms around her ribs, hugging her like I hugged that lying fucking pillow.

You are loved, it said.

I cough out a bitter, sorrowed laugh, tasting my own tears on her cold, clammy skin.

I *was* loved.

And here's the fucking proof.

Rain survived the murder-suicide of her parents, the loss of her friends and boyfriend, and the disintegration of her whole fucking town, but it was *my* neglect that finally broke her.

Just like Lily.

For the first time in my life, I think about killing myself. I could just lie down beside Rain, hold her in my arms, and with Mr. Williams's shotgun, add one more corpse to this fucked up house of death.

But I can't. That's my fucking curse. I'm a survivor.

And when I feel Rain's pulse, weak and fleeting against my cheek, I know I was right about her all along.

She's a survivor too.

CHAPTER 23

April 23
Rain

"LOOK." WES GRABS MY *arm as we cross the highway, pointing at the digital billboard above Burger Palace. "The sign is still on. What the fuck?"*

I snort and roll my eyes. "They probably have a special generator for it. God forbid we have to go a day without seeing stupid King Burger on his stupid fucking horse."

I give the animated asshole the side-eye as we approach, which he seems to return.

His cartoon eyes land on me as his deep voice booms from the loudspeakers. "What did you say, young lady?"

I look at Wes, who shrugs in response, and then back at the digital sign.

"I'm talking to yoooou!*" The ground shakes beneath my feet as King Burger points his French fry staff in my direction. It becomes three-dimensional and a thousand times longer, extending out of the screen and stopping inches away from my face.*

"I ... I'm sorry," I say, glancing up the length of the French fry at the raging monarch above.

"I will not tolerate profanity in my kingdom!"

I open my mouth to apologize again, but when I do, King Burger shoves his French fry staff right down my throat.

"Get those foul words out of your mouth," he bellows as I gag and cough and gasp for air.

It's not until I'm puking all over the sidewalk that he finally lets up.

"There you go." His voice is kinder now. Softer. "Get it all out."

I puke again, but this time, when I open my eyes, I'm hovering over a toilet bowl in a dark room. Someone is rubbing my back.

He's saying things like, "I'm so sorry," and, "That's my girl."

It sounds like Wes, but before I can turn to look at him, he shoves two fingers down my throat and makes me hurl again.

I swat at him, but my hands hit nothing. Wes evaporates like smoke, leaving me alone and on my knees. I'm no longer hugging a toilet. I'm in the woods, kneeling in wet pine straw and staring down into the watery entrance of the flooded bomb shelter. As my stomach gives one last heave, I reach into my mouth and pull something long and silky from the depths of my stomach. It just keeps coming, yard after yard. Once it's finally out, I spread it over the ground to see it better.

But I already know what it is.

A black-and-red banner.

With a demonic silhouetted horseman in the center.

And a date at the top.

Today's date.

I swing my head left and right, listening for hooves, looking for Wes. But I don't find him in the forest. I find him when I look back down at my reflection.

Is that what I look like? *I wonder, reaching up to touch my stubbly jaw, but my reflection doesn't copy me.*

Instead, it beats on the surface of the murky water with a closed fist, eyes wide and full of panic.

"Wes!" I reach out to touch his face in the water, but the surface is as smooth and hard as glass. I pound on it with both hands, but they bounce right off.

Wes's eyes are pleading. Huge bubbles leave his mouth and break against the barrier between us as he tries to tell me something.

"Wes! Hang on!" I wrap the banner around my fist and punch as hard as I can, but my blows land like pillows against the unbreakable water.

As I stop to catch my breath, I realize that Wes isn't fighting anymore. His face is calm now, and his eyes are full of remorse and acceptance.

"No!" I scream at him, pounding the surface again. "No, Wes! Fight!"

But he doesn't. He presses a hand to the glass as his face sinks away from me. His eyes lift to something over my shoulder just before they disappear into the black.

I don't have to turn around to know what he was looking at. I can feel the horse's hot, hellish breath on the back of my neck. I bow my head, ready to accept my fate, and feel the wind from a swinging mace ruffle my hair. I squeeze my eyes shut and brace for impact, but the spiked ball doesn't connect with my skull.

It shatters the glass beneath my hands.

Without thinking, I plunge into the cold, murky water, looking, reaching, grasping for Wes. But I can't find him. I swim deeper but never hit bottom. I swim to the left and right but never find a wall. I don't come up for air until my lungs begin to burn. I kick furiously to get back to the surface, clenching my teeth and holding my nose to keep from inhaling water in my desperation to breathe, but just as I prepare to crest the top of the water, I hit my head on it instead.

No!

Looking up, I pound on the glassy surface, sucking in lungfuls of water as the mace-wielding horseman watches me drown. From this angle, I can see that he does have a face under that hood after all.

A beautiful one with soft green eyes and full, smirking lips.

I bolt upright, clutching my chest and gasping for air. Every breath makes my raw throat sting. When I open my eyes, I find myself staring at a toilet. My toilet. There's a pillow on the floor by the door, which is letting a little bit of daylight in around the edges. A few candles on the counter provide the rest of the light. I recognize them from my room.

I rub my pounding temples as I try to figure out how I ended up on the bathroom floor.

The smell of vomit lingering under the vanilla is my first clue.

The man watching me from the bathtub is my second.

Wes is lying down in the tub, fully clothed. His muddy boots are propped up on the ledge, and his head is on the opposite corner. His eyelids are heavy, like I just woke him up, but his blown-out pupils are alert and trained on me.

He doesn't say anything at first, and neither do I. We just stare at each other, both waiting for the hammer to drop, and when we finally speak, it's at the exact same time.

"You slept almost all day," Wes says.

"You're really here," I blurt out.

Wes nods, and the look on his face isn't happy.

It's sad and sympathetic.

Reality wraps around my empty stomach and crushes it like an aluminum can as the meaning behind that look takes hold.

"You saw," I whisper.

Wes nods again, pressing his lips into a hard line. "I'm so sorry, Rain. About everything, but ... fuck. I just ... I had no idea."

"I'm so sorry." His words hit me like an ice-cold bucket of reality.

My chin buckles as my gaze drifts over to one of the candles. I stare at the flame until I convince myself that that's why my eyes are burning.

I'm so sorry makes it real. The way he's looking at me right now makes it real. The fact that he saw it too makes it real.

I reach into the neck of my flannel, desperate for something to shut down the pain, but my shirt has been ripped wide open, and my pills are long gone.

Because I took them all.

And *he* made me throw them up.

Grief and shame and irrational rage blur my vision and turn my hands into fists. I was going to die without ever having to feel this. Without ever having to miss them. I was going to stay numb and distracted until April 23 and then the horsemen would take me to wherever they had gone and we'd be together again like it never happened. I had a plan, but then Wes showed up and ruined everything. Now he's here and he's saying he's sorry and he's looking at me like my parents are dead and my painkillers are gone and it all hurts so fucking much and—

"I hate you!" I shout. The words echo off the walls, and tears blur my vision, so I squeeze my eyes shut and scream it again, "I hate you!"

I grab a hairbrush off the counter and throw it as hard as I can at him. Wes catches it just before it hits him in the face.

"You ruined everything! I hate you! I hate you! I hate you!"

"I know," he says, deflecting a toothbrush holder and a bottle of soap. "I'm so sorry, Rain."

"Stop saying that!"

I lunge toward the bathtub, hoping to claw his stupid green eyes out. The same ones that watched me drown in my nightmare. The same ones that are watching me drown now. But Wes grabs my wrists as I come across the edge of the bathtub and pulls me in with him.

I land on his chest, and his solid arms lock around me, pinning me in place.

"Let me go!" I howl, writhing in his grasp and kicking the tub with my bare feet. "Don't touch me! Let me go!"

But Wes just holds me tighter, shushing me like a child. I struggle and fight and kick and flail, but when I feel his lips press against the top of my head, when I feel his arms rock me from side to side, all the anger leaves my body.

In the form of a sob.

"Shh ..." Wes runs a hand over my hair, and it reminds me of the way my mom used to do it before she left for work.

I picture her exactly the way she looked the morning before it happened. Stressed. Frazzled. Her dirty-blonde hair gathered in a lopsided ponytail. Her blue hospital scrubs stained with coffee.

"Mom, we have less than a week left. Why are you still going to work? Will you please just stay home? Please? I hate being here with Dad. He just drinks and takes those painkillers for his back and messes with his guns all day. He doesn't even talk to me anymore. I think he's, like, snapped or something."

"Rainbow, we've talked about this. Not everything is about you. Other people need me, too. Now more than ever."

"I know, but—"

"No buts. There are two types of people in this world, honey— wallowers and workers. When the going gets tough, I deal with it by working, by trying to help. Which type of person are you going to be? Are you going to stay home all day and wallow, like your father, or are you gonna get out there and try to help somebody?"

"I want to help," I said, dropping my eyes to her scuffed white sneakers.

"Good. Because, when this thing blows over—and I'm sure it will— a lot of people are going to need your help."

Even though it hurts to remember her, it's also surprisingly comforting. It's almost like she's right here with me. I can still hear her voice, still smell the hazelnut-flavored coffee on her breath as she kissed my cheek. The worst part isn't seeing her again; the worst part is knowing that she's been here the whole time, but I've kept her locked away.

She deserves to be remembered.

Even if it's only for a few more hours.

When my cries die down and I finally catch my breath, Wes runs a soothing hand down my back.

"Better?" he asks, his voice barely above a whisper.

I nod, surprised to find that I actually mean it. My parents might be gone, and tomorrow might not exist, but here, in this bathtub, with the one person who came back for me, I do feel a little bit better.

"You wanna tell me what happened?"

With my cheek on his chest and my eyes lost in the flickering candlelight, I nod again. I want to get it out of me. I want to finally be free.

"I ... I couldn't sleep that night, so I snuck outside to smoke one of my dad's cigarettes. I had a few stashed in my dresser, and I thought it might help calm my nerves. He'd gotten so paranoid about the rioters and the dog attacks that I knew he'd flip out if he saw me going outside that late, so I was super quiet. I even smoked out in the tree house because I was afraid he'd see me on the porch."

I take a deep breath and focus on the rhythm of Wes's heartbeat beneath my cheek. "Just as I was finishing my cigarette, I heard a gunshot. It was so loud; it sounded like it came from inside the house, but I thought that was crazy. Then, I heard another one."

"Your room," Wes says, stroking my hair. "I saw the hole blasted in your bed when I carried you in here last night."

I nod, staring at nothing. "He thought I was asleep under the covers, like her."

I lift a shaking hand to my mouth and then still when I realize I'm not holding a cigarette. I can almost feel the grass slashing at my bare legs as I flew across the backyard and around to the front of the house, grabbing the handle on the front door as the third blast went off.

"I saw it happen." I squeeze my eyes shut, trying to stop the flow of fresh tears. "I saw my dad—"

Wes wraps his arms around me tighter and begins rocking me from side to side again.

"And, when I called my mom's name, she didn't answer ..." I catch my sobs in my flannel-covered hand, remembering the way she looked before I pulled the quilt over her head. I kissed her goodnight over the covers and told myself that she was just sleeping. That they were both just sleeping.

Then, I shut the door, polished off a bottle of cough syrup, and I went to sleep, too.

"I'm so sorry," Wes whispers into my hair.

There are those words again. *I'm so sorry.*

But, for some reason, when Wes says them this time, they don't hurt.

They help.

CHAPTER 24

Wes

I LEAD RAIN DOWN the stairs and out the back door with my hand over her eyes and my stomach in knots.

"Can I look now?"

"Not yet," I say, guiding her off the patio and into the knee-high grass.

We walk about thirty feet until we're standing in the shade of a giant oak tree on the right side of the property.

Last night, once I was sure that Rain didn't have anything left to throw up, I didn't know what the fuck to do with myself. I couldn't sleep in that house. I couldn't stand to be in there a second longer than I had to with those fucking corpses just a few rooms away. And knowing that Rain was going to have to face all that as soon as she woke up … completely sober, I knew I had to do something before I lost my shit.

I just hope it was the right thing.

With a deep breath, I uncover her eyes. "Okay. You can look now."

Even though I spent all night and most of the day on it, the job isn't pretty. The graves are shallow and the mounds are muddy and the crosses are made from sticks fastened together with grass, but at least I got those fuckers out of her house and into the dirt where they belong.

I chew on my bottom lip as I watch Rain open her eyes. After everything she's been through, the last thing I want to do is hurt her more, but when she covers her mouth and nose with her hands and looks up at me, it's not tears of pain I see in her big blue eyes. It's tears of gratitude.

I pull her against me, feeling every bit the same way. She's here, and she's okay. Even though I might only have her for a few more hours, or even minutes, every single second feels like an answered prayer.

The first one in my entire fucking life.

Prayer. That reminds me …

"Do you want to say anything?" I ask, kissing the top of her head.

She nods against my chest and lifts her glassy eyes to mine. "Thank you," she says, and the sincerity in her voice cuts me to the fucking core. "I don't … I can't believe you did all this. For *me*."

I smile and brush a tear away from her cheek with my thumb. "I'm beginning to realize there's not much I *wouldn't* do for you."

That makes Rain smile, too. "Like what?"

"What wouldn't I do for you?"

She nods, a glimmer of mischief returning to her sad red eyes.

"I don't know … piss on Tom Hanks if he were on fire?"

Rain snorts out a snotty laugh and covers her nose with the crook of her elbow as she giggles. It's the most adorable thing I've ever seen. As I watch her, I try to commit every sound, every freckle, every eyelash to memory. I know it's stupid. I know I can't take these memories with me any more than I can take her, but I hang on anyway.

If the horsemen want her, they're going to have to pry her out of my cold, dead hands.

When her laughter dies down, I gesture toward the graves with a flick of my chin. "I meant, is there anything you want to say to *them?*"

"Oh." Rain's face falls as she turns to look at the twin mounds of dirt again. "No," she says with a heartbroken yet somehow hopeful look on her face. "I'll tell them in person when I see them again."

I nod, hoping that time comes later rather than sooner.

"So, what do we do now?" Rain sniffles, looking around. "What's the new plan?"

"My only plan is to sit in that tree house"—I point in the direction of the wooden box a few yards away—"watch the sun set with this super-hot girl I kidnapped a few days ago, and then maybe make her dinner. I saw that this place has spaghetti and pancake syrup."

Rain pulls her thin, dark eyebrows together. "You mean, you're just ... giving up?"

"No," I say, taking her by the hand and leading her toward our home away from fucked up home. "I've just had a change of priorities; that's all."

"What could you possibly prioritize over surviving?" Rain asks, becoming eye-level with me as she steps onto the first rung of the tree-house ladder.

"Living." I smile.

Then, I lean forward and kiss my girl while I still can.

CHAPTER 25

Rain

LIVING.

The moment Wes's lips touch mine, I understand exactly what he means. All the death—both past and future—falls away, and there's only him. My *living*, breathing present.

I'm overwhelmed with love for him. I love him for coming back for me. I love him for saving my life even though I only have a few hours of it left. I love him for doing for my parents what I was too weak to do myself.

"I love you," I whisper against his lips, needing to say it out loud. Needing him to hear it.

Wes doesn't respond at first. He simply closes his eyes and presses his forehead to mine. Whatever he's about to say feels important, so I hold my breath as he takes one big enough for the both of us.

"The moment I saw you, I knew I was fucked." His voice is raspy and low. "I knew it when I used my last bullet to pull you out of Burger Palace instead of saving it. I knew it when I pulled that stupid fucking stunt with the dogs instead of leaving you at Huckabee Foods. I knew it when I got shot for you, when I got a flat tire because of you, and when I went back into a burning building to find your ass. The whole time, I thought you were distracting me from my mission, but it wasn't until you left that I realized you *were* my mission." Wes opens his eyes, and his pupils drink me in. "I think I came here to find *you*, Rain. I'm just sorry it took me so long to figure that out."

"Don't be sorry," I whisper around the lump in my throat. "I'm sorry. It sounds like I've been a real pain in the ass."

Wes laughs, and the vision is so beautiful that I feel like I'm looking into the sun. I take a picture of him with my mind, the way he looks right now—backlit by an orange sky, white teeth glowing in his crescent smile, and a lock of brown hair grazing his perfect cheekbone. I want to remember this moment forever.

Even if forever is only for tonight.

"I fucking love you," he says with that perfect smile just before it crashes against mine.

I let go of the ladder and wrap my arms around Wes's neck, knowing without a shred of doubt that he won't let me fall. What I don't expect is for him to grab the backs of my thighs and wrap them around his waist in the process. It's fitting that I'm no longer attached to the earth because that's how I feel whenever I kiss Wes—supported, secure, suspended above my problems.

His tongue and teeth aren't gentle as they take what they want, and neither is his body as it presses mine against the ladder. Desperation fuels us as we bite and suck and push and pull. We have so much lost time to make up for and so little of it left to spare. April 23 is almost over, and every heartbeat that pumps through my veins is another second I've wasted not making love to this man.

I lock my ankles behind Wes's back as he reaches over my head to grab the ladder. Squeezing my eyes shut, I hold on tight as he begins to climb, never once breaking our kiss. As soon as Wes reaches the top, we become a blur of hands and zippers and shirts and skin.

I lift my ass off the plywood floor as Wes shimmies my pants and panties off. Then, I part my knees for him as he frees himself from his jeans. As he climbs over me, I reach for him, desperate for him to fill me—to make me whole again—but Wes stills and gazes down at me instead.

"What is it?" I ask, reaching up to cup his stubbled cheek.

Two deep lines have formed between his dark eyebrows. I feel mine do the same.

"Nothing. I just ... wanted to look at you ..."

One last time, his sad smile says.

I don't want to see that look, so I kiss it away as I lift my hips to let him in.

But something happens as soon as Wes and I are joined. All that time that felt like it was slipping away? It doesn't just slow down. It stops. We inhale. We exhale. We kiss. We connect. And when we finally start moving again, it's with the lazy grace of melting ice cream.

Because that's all we are.

Something to be savored before it disappears.

CHAPTER 26

Wes

"THIS IS SO NICE." *Rain sighs as she rests her head on my shoulder.*

The Franklin Springs Cinema wasn't exactly hard to break into. Now, figuring out how to work the projector, that took a minute.

"I would have taken you to dinner too, but I can't exactly afford to pay sixty-eight bucks for an Apocasized King Meal right now."

Rain giggles and pats the cardboard bucket in her lap. "I'd rather eat stale popcorn for the rest of my life than step foot in that place again."

"That's good because it might come down to that." I smile and kiss the top of her head.

It feels so fucking weird, being on a date with this girl. I mean, I've dated lots of girls, but it was always an exchange. An understood transaction. With Rain, I just ... want to make her happy.

"Aquaman?" she asks as the opening credits begin to roll.

"What? It was that or Dumbo.*"*

A flirty grin tugs at the corners of her mouth. "I'm not complaining."

"Oh, really? You gotta thing for Jason Momoa, huh?"

"No." She drops her eyes, and I can see the blush rising to her cheeks, even in the darkened auditorium. "But I might have a thing for another guy with tattoos."

"I fucking hope so," I say, pulling her into my lap as her squeals compete with the booming speakers.

When I glance back at the screen, Jason Momoa is carrying a rescued fisherman into a bar. The camera pans from a table full of fishermen to the counter where he's ordering a shot of whiskey. The movement is so fluid, so fast, that I almost miss it, but I swear, on the wall of the bar, I saw a red banner with a black horseman on it.

"Did you see that?" I ask without taking my eyes off the screen.

"See what?"

"That banner."

Rain looks around the room. "Where?"

"Not here." I point to the screen. "In the movie."

"Really?"

I set her on her feet and stand up. "We should go."

"Why? We just got here."

"Because ..." I gesture toward the screen as Jason Momoa snatches the bottle from the bartender and begins to chug. Then, I do a double take. The label on the bottle reads April 23. *"Rain! Look!"*

But, by the time she swings her head toward the screen, Jason has already smashed the bottle on the ground.

"Wes, I don't see anything."

"I think that's the point."

I grab her hand and sprint out of the auditorium and toward the main exit. The second we enter the lobby, four black-and-red banners unfurl from the ceiling, separating us from our escape. We're running too fast to stop, so I sweep my arm out to push one aside ... and watch the image of the horseman dissolve into tiny pixels of light around my hand. I turn around, but from behind, it looks just as real as the others.

"Wes, come on!"

Rain is tugging on my arm, but I barely feel it as I stare at the back of the floor-to-ceiling strip of fabric. Reaching out, I run my fingers along the surface again. I feel absolutely nothing as they pass through, leaving a digital trail of multicolored pixels in their wake.

"Look." I do it again, this time sticking my whole arm through. "It's not real."

"Is that real?" The terror in her voice grabs my attention.

I swing my head around as the double doors burst open, and a smoke-spewing horse from hell charges through. The faceless, hooded motherfucker on his back swings his steel sword over his head in a flourish of swoops. I manage to push Rain out of the way before he strikes, closing my eyes and bracing for impalement, but when his blade slices through me, it feels like nothing more than a whoosh of air.

By the time I open my eyes, the horseman, the banners, all of it is gone.

It's just me and Rain and a profound revelation.

None of this is real.

When I open my eyes, it takes me a minute to remember where I am. It's dark outside, and I'm sore as fuck—both from digging graves all day and from sleeping on a plywood floor.

And probably from a few of the positions I twisted Rain into before I passed out.

I sit up and find her sitting with her back against the wall of the tree house and her legs straight out in front of her. She's staring out the entrance, lost in thought. That is, until I stretch and five different joints all crack at once.

She jumps and turns toward me, her shoulders sagging in relief a moment later. "I was wondering when you were gonna wake up."

"I didn't even realize I'd fallen asleep," I grumble, rubbing the back of my neck. "How long was I out?"

"I don't know. An hour, maybe two?"

"And still no horsemen, huh?"

Rain shakes her head. "I've been hearing gunshots in the distance but no hooves. This shit is killing me, Wes. It wasn't so bad when you were awake and ..." She drops her eyes, and I can almost see her blush in the dark. "But, the whole time you were asleep, I've just been sitting here, waiting for the world to end. Why hasn't it happened yet? What the fuck are they waiting for?" Her voice cracks at the end, and I know it won't be long before she cracks, too.

I crawl over to her and kiss her worried brow. "I had a dream just now; it was like the nightmare, but ... I think it was trying to tell me something. Come on." I kiss her again before climbing down the ladder.

"No, Wes! Where are you going?" she shrieks, peering down at me. The whites of her wide eyes almost glow in the dark as they jerk left and right, looking for any sign of danger.

"I'm going to prove to you that there's nothing to be afraid of. Come on."

Rain climbs down the ladder on trusting, trembling legs and holds my hand like a vise as we walk across the yard. The sounds of faraway gunshots and howling dogs and shattering glass tell me that I might have spoken too soon. Just because the horsemen aren't real doesn't change the fact that the whole world has lost its goddamn mind.

We still have plenty to be afraid of.

I pull the flashlight from my pocket and light our way as we enter through the back door, careful not to shine it anywhere near the mangled recliner. I lead Rain upstairs and feel her sweaty palm begin to shake in my grasp.

God, I hope I'm right.

We head into her room where she immediately shuts and locks the door behind us. Her hands are covering the lower half of her face, and it looks like she's on the verge of hysterics.

"Wes, just tell me what the hell is going on! Please!"

I grab her phone off the nightstand and swipe it open as quickly as possible. "I have to show you."

"The cell towers are down, remember? There's no service."

"You were listening to music earlier," I say, hunting for the app.

"Just what I have saved on my phone."

There.

I press the blue music note icon and find what I'm looking for. Turning the screen toward Rain, I point to the little black dot I noticed last night when I paused that incessant fucking song.

She crosses the room and stares at it in confusion.

"That's just a blown-out pixel." The screen illuminates the disappointment on her face.

"Maybe."

I turn the phone back around and take a screenshot of the music app. Using the camera tool, I zoom in on the image as much as I can. Then, I save it and zoom in on the second version even more. Sure enough, once it's large enough, the blip takes on the unmistakable silhouette that's been haunting our dreams for almost a year.

Rain's mouth falls open as she sees the image take shape. "What does it mean?"

"It means someone's fucking with us." I begin opening and closing every app on her phone, searching for more abnormalities. It doesn't take long to find another one. "Shit."

"What?"

I turn the phone toward her. "Open Instagram and pay attention to what you see before the feed comes up." I watch her face as a red light splashes across it. "Did you see it?"

Her eyes are two perfect circles as they lift back to mine. "Was that the banner?"

"It flashed too fast to be sure, but I know it was red and black."

Rain sits on the bed next to me and stares at the floor, taking it all in. "So, you're saying somebody's been *planting* these images in our heads?"

I nod, feeling sick to my stomach. "Subliminal messaging. And this is just what we can find on your phone. I'm sure we were being exposed to way more through TVs and tablets and—"

"Billboards."

Rain and I lock eyes as we try to make sense of our new reality.

"Who would do this?" she asks.

"I don't know. Could be anyone from a couple of hackers on a power trip to some third-world dictator trying to destroy modernized society."

"So, does this mean the apocalypse isn't coming? It was all just a sick joke to make us go crazy?"

I illuminate the screen on her phone again, turning it toward her so that she can see the clock for herself. "Considering that it's after midnight, I think it's safe to say that the apocalypse isn't coming."

"April twenty-*fourth*." Her voice is barely a whisper as I watch her face go through the entire range of human emotion, illuminated by the digital glow. Relief. Elation. Grief. Regret. Then, as the sound of approaching destruction begins to rise in the distance, pure, unfiltered dread.

The sound is like a never-ending car accident—metal scraping metal, crunching glass, and squealing steel.

And it's getting closer.

"Pack your shit and get ready to run," I snap, thrusting the phone into her hand. "Does your dad have any more guns?"

She nods blankly. "In the master closet."

I run across the hall with my flashlight, holding my breath to cope with the lingering stench of death in the room. Throwing open the closet door, I shine my light in all directions, not knowing where to look. There are scrubs and shoes and suits and dresses and—

Bingo.

The light lands on a black briefcase sitting on the floor next to the door—the kind that takes a code to open. Luckily, I have the code—in the form of a pocketknife. Jamming my blade underneath the brass plate, I pop the case open in three seconds flat, and the sight inside takes my breath away.

A Smith & Wesson .44 Magnum. Six-inch barrel. Black with a wooden grip.

Rain's dad must have been a *Dirty Harry* fan.

I lift the beast out of the molded foam cutout it's nestled into and check the cylinder.

And it's fully fucking loaded.

I shake my head in disbelief and kiss the barrel before tucking it into my holster.

For some reason, God likes me today. I hope I don't fuck it up.

When I get back to Rain's room, she's kneeling in front of her open window, gripping the ledge as she waits for whatever the fuck is coming. Her backpack is on her shoulders, almost bursting, and I can see that she's wearing a hoodie underneath it.

I cross the room and lean against the wall next to the window. "That sweatshirt had better not have a Twenty One Pilots logo on it." I smirk.

Rain looks up at me with fear carved into her beautiful face. "*That's* what you're thinking about right now?"

From here, I can see that the sweatshirt says *Franklin Springs High.*

Thank fuck.

I bend over and kiss her worried, wrinkled little forehead. "Try to relax, okay? The horsemen aren't real. Whatever is coming, it's human. And, if it's human"—I pull the left side of my Hawaiian shirt open to show her my newest acquisition—"we can kill it."

Rain's shoulders sag as she gives me a brave nod. "Sit."

She pats the carpet, and I notice a fresh bandage, antibiotic ointment, a pill, and a glass of water laid out on a paper towel beside her.

The sight makes me feel like I've been punched in the heart.

"Wes?"

I bite my lip and try to focus on the grinding, crashing, squealing noises approaching outside and not the stinging sensation behind my eyes.

"Baby, are you okay?"

Baby.

I've never been anybody's fucking baby, not even when I *was* a baby. But, for some fucked up reason that I don't understand, I'm hers. Maybe, one day, being treated like I matter won't hurt so goddamn much, but I hope not. I hope it guts me every time, forever, as a reminder that this girl is a fucking miracle.

"Yeah," I whisper, clearing my throat as I drop to my knees beside her.

Rain gives me a shy smile as she goes to work on my arm, jumping a little from the grinding, gnashing, crashing sounds getting closer outside. I pop the Keflex into my mouth and swallow it without taking my eyes off her.

"Why are you staring at me like that?" she asks, looking up at me through her long, dark lashes.

"Because I fucking love you."

The smile on her face lights up the dark room. It's the prettiest thing I've ever seen, and I suddenly can't wait for whatever is coming to get here so that I can kill it and turn its teeth into jewelry for her to wear.

Especially when another crash makes her gasp and cover that beautiful smile with both hands.

We look back outside as lights illuminate the highway. The overturned Corolla to the right of the driveway begins to lurch and move, scraping across the asphalt as Rain's eyes lift to mine.

"Listen to me." I cup her face in my hands, stealing her attention. Commanding it. "The horsemen aren't real. Do you hear me? Whatever that is, people are behind it. People who are gonna fucking die if they try to hurt a hair on your head."

Rain nods as the lurching sedan at the end of her driveway rolls sideways and takes out her mailbox. We both turn at the same time, watching as the force behind the shove comes into view.

"Is that a—"

"Bulldozer!" Rain takes off like a shot.

I grab my flashlight and take off after her, but by the time I make it downstairs, the front door is already wide open.

"Fuck! Rain, stop!"

I don't catch up to her until she's almost at the end of her driveway, jumping up and down and waving her arms. The bulldozer slows down as I dart in front of her, shoving her behind my back and grabbing the revolver under my arm.

"Well, got-damn!" a voice shouts from the cabin of the idling machine.

I shine my flashlight toward it and find Quinton and Lamar—the brothers from the hardware store—shielding their eyes from the beam.

I lower the light but keep my hand on my gun.

"You got it working!" Rain yells, jumping up and down behind me.

"I told y'all we weren't gonna get no damn flat!" Lamar shouts over the snarling engine.

"Finally got the damn thing up and runnin'," Quinton adds, "and none too soon. Rednecks in town done lost their damn minds."

"We're getting the fuck outta here," Lamar adds. "Y'all comin'?"

"Yes!" Rain shouts, peeking out from around my arm.

Quinton gives her a little salute, and I don't know if I want to blow his head off for looking at her like that or pat him on the back for making her so damn happy. Personally, I don't give a shit if we stay or go. As long as Rain is with me, we could live in a hollowed-out tree for all I fucking care. Supplies, shelter, self-defense—those are just icing on the vanilla-flavored cake now.

"We'll be right behind ya." I holster my gun and give the guys a nod.

I don't trust them—I don't trust anybody with a dick around my girl—but the survivor in me recognizes a good resource when it sees one.

I follow Rain as she tears back into the house, flying through the kitchen and into the garage. I shine the light ahead of me as I step into the musty, humid space and find a very excited Rain standing next to a very badass Kawasaki Ninja.

"Do you know how to drive it?" she asks, the contents of her backpack jostling with every bounce. "My mom never taught me."

"Fuck yeah, I do." I grin.

Rain runs over to the wall and grabs the keys off a hook while I shine the light above us, finding the emergency release latch for the garage door. I pull the red handle and then walk over and shove the heavy-ass door all the way up. The scraping and crashing of Quinton and Lamar's bulldozer clearing the highway fills the garage, but it doesn't sound like hell anymore.

To Rain, it sounds like heaven.

When I turn around, she's watching me, holding a black helmet and grinning with that wild, impulsive look in her eye. That look usually ends with me almost getting killed trying to save her ass, but I don't mind anymore. In fact, I have a feeling that's why I'm here.

Rain holds the helmet out to me, so I take it.

And shove it onto her head.

And kiss the visor with a smile.

Rain climbs on behind me and holds on tight as I fire up the Ninja. It purrs like a fucking kitten and has almost a full tank of gas.

Looking skyward, I say a silent, *Thank you,* as I twist the throttle, launching us out of the garage and onto the midnight highway beyond.

Rain squeals in delight, giving the house of horrors her middle finger as we pass.

I might not know where we're going or what we'll find when we get there, but I do know that, whatever it is, it's gonna have to go through me to get to her.

Me and my new pal, God.

To Be Continued ...

Read on for a sneak peek at Chapter 1 of
Fighting for Rain, *coming this fall!*

CHAPTER 1

April 24
Rain

WITH MY ARMS AROUND Wes's waist and the roar of a
motorcycle engine drowning out my thoughts, I turn and
watch my house disappear behind us. My home. The only one
I've ever known. The trees and darkness swallow it whole, but
they don't take my memories of what happened there. I wish
they would. I wish I could pull this ache out of my chest and
throw it into that house like a hand grenade.

I also wish I weren't wearing this damn motorcycle helmet.
Wes should be wearing it. He's the survivalist. I don't really
care if my head gets cracked open. All I want to do is lay my
cheek on Wes's back and let the wind dry my tears. Besides,
the inside of it smells like hazelnut coffee and cold-cream
moisturizer.

Just like my mom.

Who's now buried in a shallow grave in our backyard.

Right beside the man who killed her.

I might have survived April 23—the apocalypse that never
happened—but not all of me made it out alive. Rainbow
Williams—the perfect, blonde, straight A–earning, church-
going girlfriend of Franklin Springs High School basketball star
Carter Renshaw—is buried back there, too, right next to the
parents she was trying so hard to please.

All that's left of me now is Rain.

Whoever the hell that is.

I curl my fingers into Wes's blue Hawaiian shirt and look over his shoulder at the black highway laid out before us. My friends, Quint and Lamar, are up ahead in their daddy's bulldozer, clearing a path through all the wrecked and abandoned vehicles that piled up during the chaos before April 23, but it's so dark that I can barely see them. All I can see is the road directly in front of our headlight and a few sparks in the distance where the bulldozer's blade is grinding against the asphalt. All I can smell are my memories. All I can feel is Wes's warm body in my arms and a sense of freedom in my soul, growing with every mile we put between us and Franklin Springs.

And, right now, that's all I need.

The rumble of the road and the emotional exhaustion of the past few days have me fighting to keep my eyes open. I nod off I don't know how many times as we crawl along behind the bulldozer, jerking awake the moment I feel that first twitch of sleep.

Wes slows to a stop so that he can turn to face me. A lock of hair falls over one cheek, but the rest is pushed straight back and tangled from the wind. His pale green eyes are almost the only feature I can make out in the dark. And they don't look too happy.

"You're scaring the shit out of me. You've got to try to stay awake, okay?" Wes shouts over the sound of metal scraping asphalt up ahead.

I glance past him and see the headlights of the bulldozer shining on the roof of an overturned eighteen-wheeler. It's blocking the entire highway, but Quint and Lamar are hard at work, trying to push it out of our path.

I pull the helmet off my head and feel my mother disappear along with her scent. It's replaced with the smell of spring pollen, pine trees, and gasoline.

"I know," I shout back with a guilty nod. "I'm trying."

A burst of sparks flies behind Wes as the bulldozer gives the tractor-trailer another good shove.

Wes puts the kickstand down and gets off the bike. "This is gonna take them a while. Maybe you should stand up and walk around a little. Might help you wake up."

He's just a silhouette, backlit by the haze from the headlight, but he's still the most beautiful thing I've ever seen—tall and strong and smart and *here*, even after everything he just saw. As I place my palm in his, the tiny orange sparkles of light glittering in the background match the ones dancing across my skin, giving me goose bumps, even under my hoodie.

I can't see his expression, but I feel Wes smiling down at me. Then, suddenly, his energy shifts. As I slide off the bike, he grips my hand tighter, lifting his head and inhaling so deeply that I can hear it, even over the grinding, crunching sounds coming from the bulldozer.

"Shit." The profile of his perfect face comes into view as he turns his head to look over his shoulder. "I think I smell—"

Before the word can even leave Wes's lips, the eighteen-wheeler explodes in a ball of fire. White-hot light fills my eyes and scorches my face as Wes tackles me to the ground.

I don't feel the impact. I don't hear the debris landing all around us. I don't even hear my own voice as I shout my friends' names. All I can hear are the thoughts in my head, telling me to get up. To run. To help.

Wes is looking down at me now. His lips are moving, but I can't tell what he's saying. Another explosion goes off, and I cover my face. When I lower my hands, he's gone.

I sit up and see Wes's silhouette running toward the bulldozer.

Which is now engulfed in flames.

"Quint!" I scream, taking off in a sprint toward the passenger side as Wes heads toward the driver's side. "Lamar!"

I climb up onto the track, thanking God that the fire hasn't made it through the blown-out windshield yet, and pull the door open. Inside, Quint and Lamar are slumped over in their seats, covered in broken glass. Wes is unbuckling Quint's seat belt.

Wes's head snaps up when I open the door, and his dark eyebrows pull together. "I told you to stay the fuck there!"

"I couldn't hear you!" I lean into the cab, struggling to move Lamar's body so that I can unbuckle his seat belt.

"Rain, stop!" Wes snaps at me as he lifts Quint's lifeless body into his arms.

"I can help!" I get the belt off and give Lamar's lifeless body a hard shake. His eyes flutter open as something begins to hiss and pop under the flaming hood. "Come on, buddy. We gotta go."

Lamar twists in his seat to try to climb out, but he winces and pulls his eyes shut again.

"Lamar," I shout, tugging on his shoulders. "I need you to walk. Right now."

His head rolls toward me, and the light from the flames illuminates a deep gash across his forehead. The dark red blood glistens against his dark brown skin. I pull on his arms harder, but he's so heavy.

"Lamar! Wake up! Please!"

Two hands clamp around my waist and pull me out of the cabin just before a blur of Hawaiian print breezes past me to take my place.

"Go!" Wes shouts as he pulls Lamar from the bulldozer. "Now!"

I jump off the track to get out of his way and run toward the motorcycle. As I get closer, I notice Quint's body lying on the ground next to it.

It isn't moving.

As I rush to him, my mind goes back to the day we met. We were in the same preschool class, and I found Quint off by himself on the first day of school, quietly eating Play-Doh behind Ms. Gibson's desk. He begged me not to tell on him. I didn't, of course. I sat and ate some with him just to see what all the fuss was about.

I found out years later that his daddy used to beat him whenever he got in trouble, so he got real good at not getting caught. His little brother, Lamar, didn't seem to learn the same lesson. He got caught all the time, but Quint always took the blame.

I kneel next to my very first friend and reach for his throat, hoping to find a pulse, but I don't get that far. I find a shard of glass sticking out of his neck instead.

"Oh my God." The words fall from my mouth as I grab his wrist, pushing and prodding and praying for a heartbeat.

Wes sets Lamar down next to me as another explosion rattles the ground below us. I scream and cover my head as the hood of the bulldozer lands with a clang about thirty feet away and skids to a stop.

Wes leans over and puts his hands on his knees to catch his breath. "He okay?" he asks, gesturing to Quint with a flick of his head.

"He's alive, but ..." I drop my eyes to the glass sticking out of his neck and shake my head. "I don't know what to do."

God, I wish my mom were here. She would know. She was an ER nurse.

Was.

Now, she's dead.

Just like we're going to be if we don't get the hell out of here before that gas tank explodes.

I look around and realize that, with the light from the flames, I can actually see where we are now. The sides of the highway are cluttered with all the cars and trucks that Quint and Lamar pushed out of our way, but the faded green exit sign on the side of the road says it all.

PRITCHARD PARK MALL

NEXT RIGHT

My eyes meet Wes's, and without saying a word, we get to work. He stashes the motorcycle in the woods, I drag the hood of the bulldozer over to make a stretcher for Quint, and Lamar shakes off his daze enough to stand and help carry his brother past the wreckage.

When we get to the exit ramp, Pritchard Park Mall sits at the bottom, shining in the moonlight like a worthless mountain of crumbling concrete. It's been rotting away ever since the last store closed up shop about ten years ago, but the land isn't valuable enough for anyone to even bother tearing it down.

"Fuck. Look at that place," Wes groans. He's holding one side of the makeshift stretcher while Lamar and I struggle with the other. "You sure about this?"

"I don't know where else to go," I huff, shifting my grip on the corner of the yellow hood. "We can't put Quint on the bike, we can't leave him here, and we can't sleep in the woods because the dogs will sniff out the food in our pack."

A howl rises over the sound of burning metal, pushing us to move faster.

"You okay, man?" Wes asks Lamar, changing the subject. He doesn't want to talk about what we might find inside this place any more than I do.

Lamar just nods, staring straight ahead. Quint's smart-ass little brother hasn't said a word since he came to, but at least he can walk. And follow directions. That's actually an improvement for him.

When we get to the bottom of the ramp, we find a chain-link fence circling the perimeter of the mall property. The sounds of gunshots, terrified screams, and revving engines fill the air—probably Pritchard City rioters, based on the direction of the noise—but they obviously don't care about looting the mall.

They're smart enough to know there's nothing left to loot.

We walk along the fence until we find a spot that's been flattened. Then, we cross the parking lot and head toward what used to be the main entrance.

We pass a few cars with For Sale signs in their broken windows, kick a few hypodermic needles along the way, and eventually make it to a row of tinted glass doors. One has been broken out already, which makes the hair on the back of my neck stand up.

We're not the first ones here.

The bulldozer hood won't fit through the door, so we set it down on the sidewalk and stare at each other.

"I'll go first," Wes says, pulling the gun from his holster.

"I'm going with you," I announce before glancing over at Lamar. "You stay with him."

But Lamar's not listening. He's staring at his big brother like he hung the moon.

And then fell from it.

"Don't you dare touch that glass," I add, pointing to Quint's neck. "He'll bleed out. Do you hear me?"

Lamar nods once but still doesn't look up.

When I turn back toward Wes, I expect him to argue with me about coming with him, but he doesn't. He simply offers his elbow for me to take and gives me a sad, exhausted, exquisite smile.

"No fight?" I ask, wrapping my hand around his tattooed bicep.

Wes kisses the top of my head. "No fight," he whispers. "I'm not letting you out of my sight."

Something in his words makes my cheeks flush. I should be afraid of walking into an abandoned mall with no electricity at night in the middle of a fake apocalypse, but as Wes tucks me behind his back and pulls the broken door open, the only thing I feel is a giddy, girlie sense of belonging. I would follow this man to the ends of the earth, and the fact that he's willing to let me only makes me love him more.

Wes guides us through the open door and eases it closed with the tiniest click. We tiptoe over the broken glass like professionals, and Wes leads the way with his gun stretched out in front of us. The shopping mall is pitch-black inside, but the sound of people talking in the distance has me gripping his arm even tighter.

I tug on his good shoulder and push up to my tiptoes so that my mouth is level with his ear. "Do you hear that?" I whisper. "It sounds like they're in the food court. Maybe, if we hide out in that first store by the entrance, they won't know we're—"

"Freeze!" a man shouts from the end of the hall.

Instinctively, I hold my hands up and step in front of Wes. "Please," I shout back even though I can't see who I'm speaking to. "Our friends outside are hurt. We just need a place to spend the night."

"Rainbow?" His voice softens, and I recognize it instantly.

It's one I've heard say my name a thousand different times in a thousand different ways. It's one I never thought I'd hear again, and after I met Wes, never wanted to. It's the voice of the boy who left me behind.

"Carter?"

I thought April twenty-fourth was going to be a new beginning.

Turns out, it's just the beginning of the end.

PLAYLIST

THIS PLAYLIST IS A collection of songs that I either mentioned in *Praying for Rain* or that I felt illustrated a feeling or a scene from the book. I am grateful to each and every one of the brilliant artists listed below. Their creativity fuels mine.

You can stream the playlist for free on Spotify: http://spoti.fi/3agDqyM.

"400 Lux" by Lorde

"Alone Together" by Fall Out Boy

"Baby" by Bishop Briggs

"Black Wave" by K. Flay

"Cut Yr Teeth" by Kississippi

"Dark Blue" by Jack's Mannequin

"Eurotrash Girl" by Cracker

"Guns for Hands" by Twenty One Pilots

"Hard Times (Acoustic)" by Guster

"Hold On" by Flor

"Heavydirtysoul" by Twenty One Pilots

"I Know Places" by Taylor Swift

"I'm With You" by Vance Joy

"Little Heaven" by Toad the Wet Sprocket

"Love Story" by G-Eazy & Halsey

"My Blood" by Twenty One Pilots

"On Your Porch" by The Format

"Stolen" by Dashboard Confessional

"Twinkle" by Whipping Boy

"Wrestle Yü to Hüsker Dü" by The Dirty Nil

"You Can't Look Back" by Taking Back Sunday

BOOKS BY BB EASTON

ROM-COM MEMOIR

The inspiration for Sex/Life, a steamy dramedy series coming soon to Netflix!

44 Chapters About 4 Men

THE 44 CHAPTERS SPIN-OFF SERIES

Darkly funny. Deeply emotional. Shockingly sexy.

SKIN (Knight's backstory, Book 1)
SPEED (Harley's backstory, Book 2)
STAR (Hans's backstory, Book 3)
SUIT (Ken's backstory, Book 4)

THE RAIN TRILOGY

A gritty, suspenseful, dystopian love story.

Praying for Rain
Fighting for Rain
Dying for Rain

ACKNOWLEDGMENTS

Ken, thank you for helping me name this book and for pretending to listen when I brainstormed out loud at you and for making dinner all those times I was too deep in the writing cave to emerge before sundown and for doing my taxes and making my spreadsheets and for not leaving me for **Colleen Hoover** (yet). You're the best husbot a girl could have, and if the apocalypse ever comes, I know we'll be okay, thanks to your insistence on buying everything in bulk.

To **my mother and mother-in-law**—Thank you for never hesitating to watch my children so that I can traipse all over the globe, chasing this delicious dream. Your love and support know no bounds, and neither does my gratitude for you.

To my content editors, **Karla Nellenbach** and **Traci Finlay**, and my copy editors, **Jovana Shirley** and **Ellie McLove**— This book scared the hell out of me. I felt a lot like Wes as I wrote it, fumbling through unfamiliar places in the dark, waiting for some new problem to jump out and fuck up my plans. Thank you for guiding me through it with your expert hands. I appreciate and admire you women so much.

To my beta readers and proofreaders, **Tracey Frazier, April C., Sara Snow, Sammie Lynn, Rhonda Lind, Michelle Beiger DePrima, and Sarah Plocher**—Thank you for always at least pretending to be excited about my new projects and for putting your lives on hold to read them for me. I almost want to get married again so that you can all be my bridesmaids. I love you guys!

To my publicist, **Jenn Watson,** and the rest of the team at **Social Butterfly PR**—Thank you for spreading the word about this book, keeping me organized and sane(ish), and showering me with cupcakes, Sharpies, cough drops, and Advil at my signings. You guys are absolute rock stars. (I should know—I've seen you do karaoke.)

To **Larry, Miles**, and **Jay**—Thank you for another year of dreaming big. Here's to many more!

To **Ace Gray**—Thank you for inspiring me with your hatred of Tom Hanks.

To **all my author friends**—Thanks to you, I don't have competitors; I have coworkers. I'm not isolated; I'm inundated with love and support. You share with me your time, your advice, your encouragement, your resources, and often, your platforms to help me succeed in an oversaturated market where so very few do. Thank you for letting this pink-haired, foul-mouthed, new kid sit with you. I love you!

To **the girls (and a few boys) of #TeamBB**—Thank you for the gorgeous Instagram teasers, the Facebook shares, the five-star reviews that never fail to make me cry, the thoughtful gifts, and the tireless pimping you've showered me with over the years. It is because of *you*, forcing your friends and book clubs and sisters and significant others to read my books, oftentimes under the threat of physical violence, that I've been able to pursue this dream at all. I'm humbled by your rabid, relentless support and proud to call you all friends. Thank you for *everything*. If any of you ever need a kidney, I'm your girl.

ABOUT THE AUTHOR

BB Easton lives in the suburbs of Atlanta, Georgia, with her long-suffering husband, Ken, and two adorable children. She recently quit her job as a school psychologist to write books about her punk rock past and deviant sexual history full-time. Ken is suuuper excited about that.

Praying for Rain is her first full-length work of fiction. The idea, fittingly, came to her in a dream.

If that sounds like the kind of person you want to go around being friends with, then by all means, feel free to drop her a line. You can find her procrastinating at all of the following places:

Email: authorbbeaston@gmail.com

Website: www.authorbbeaston.com

Facebook: www.facebook.com/bbeaston

Instagram: www.instagram.com/author.bb.easton

Twitter: www.twitter.com/bb_easton

Pinterest: www.pinterest.com/artbyeaston

Goodreads: https://goo.gl/4hiwiR

BookBub:
https://www.bookbub.com/authors/bb-easton

Spotify:
https://open.spotify.com/user/bbeaston

Selling signed books and original art on Etsy:
www.etsy.com/shop/artbyeaston

Giving stuff away in her #TeamBB Facebook group:
www.facebook.com/groups/BBEaston

And giving away a free e-book from one of her author friends each month in her newsletter: http://eepurl.com/c4OCOH

Made in the USA
Columbia, SC
31 May 2021

38777974R00133